I0659650

HALF MAN
HALF MISFIT

Dave Kidd

MT-ink.co.uk

First published by MT Ink in 2014

© Dave Kidd 2014

ISBN: 978-0-9929397-0-0

Dave Kidd asserts the moral right to be
identified as the author of this work

A catalogue record of this book is
available from the British Library

This is a work of fiction. Names, characters, businesses, places, events
and incidents are either the products of the author's imagination or
used in a fictitious manner. Any resemblance to actual persons, living
or dead, or actual events is purely coincidental.

The author and publisher will be happy to satisfy any copyright issues
in future editions.

All rights reserved. No part of this publication may be reproduced,
stored in a retrieval system or transmitted in any form or by any means
- electronic, mechanical, photocopying, recording or otherwise -
without the prior written permission of the publisher.

For licencing inquiries contact the publisher through MT-ink.co.uk.

In memory of Dave Warriner, a fine friend
and an outstanding drinking partner…

CONTENTS

1

THE HAPPIEST PERSON
IN THE WORLD

The happiest person in the world has just taken delivery of the Young Fresh Fellows CD *This One's For The Ladies*, an album he has not listened to for a decade, since he threw out his last vinyl turntable. Having tracked down the CD on import and having had it shipped from the United States at no little expense, he has inserted the disc into a portable CD player and forwarded it immediately to track nine, *Taco Wagon*, to which he is now gleefully playing air guitar, having forgotten quite how good a track this was.

At the climactic moment when the only lyrics – 'Taco Wagon!' – are first yelled, he officially becomes the happiest person in the world, as measured by the Worldwide Happiness Index, having just overtaken a fisherman from Barbados who is blessed with an astonishing level of inner serenity so high that it is only perceptible to dogs. The happiest person in the world is unaware of his newfound status and, had he known, he would instantly have lost top spot, by virtue of the level of guilt he would have felt, due to his fundamental decency.

Again, unbeknown to him, he has registered in the top one hundred happiest of the planet's seven billion people, for every moment of the past two years. The index calculates happiness by a cumulative measure, of course. The happiest man is not permanently orgasmic. That would be ridiculous. It's just that the first scream of *Taco Wagon*! happened to be the precise moment when he overtook our serene Bajan angler, by a tiny fraction some way east of the decimal point.

Ever since the masterstroke decision of the British Government to introduce a Happiness Index, the instigation of a worldwide version was only going to be a matter of time. We won't go into the advanced mathematics of it all. The maths are not important. It's not as if our friend in Barbados has suddenly become miserable, after all.

And we'd all gladly take a position in the world's top million, even hundred million. No, the importance lies in the factors which are making this man so extremely happy.

On a micro level, it helps that he doesn't illegally download music. Had he illegally downloaded 'Taco Wagon' by the Young Fresh Fellows, he would have felt no great satisfaction in hearing such a long-lost gem. The online tracking-down of this obscure CD, the payment of a relatively substantial sum and the fact that his purchase had temporarily slipped out of his mind, had made its arrival such a significant high. And this for a man who, as we know, has already been consistently happy for a remarkable period of time.

The macro level, though, is what you will almost certainly be more interested in. And perhaps the most pertinent fact is that the happiest 1,467,250 people on Earth are all male. Inherent levels of female respon-sibility, and their accompanying guilt, play a significant part here. Then there's the fact that should a woman suddenly realise that she has become unfeasibly happy, she would instantly wonder whether the woman who lives across the street was even happier still. The other woman is slimmer, after all.

The Index states that women are far less capable of reaching extreme levels of happiness by virtue of such apparent trivialities as the rediscovery of a magnificent, little-known record from the Pacific North-West, nor by the result of a sporting contest nor, say, by the taste of real ale (statistically the most pleasurable drink in the world, which is one reason Englishmen are so prominent in the upper reaches of the Index).

Anyway, enough of gender politics. You doubtless want to know exactly what makes this particular man tick.

Well, he's 38 years old, which is the optimum age for happiness. Through experience, he has assumed absolute self-confidence but, personally, he is too young to worry about death.

In terms of money, he just about registers as one of the top three per cent of England's most wealthy. Rich enough to have everything he feels he needs, better off than his significant family and his oldest friends - but not by so great a margin that they have started hating him as a result.

He works – but, here's the thing, he actually works for only around two to three hours a week.

Employed by a leading advertising agency as a slogan writer, he is allowed to work from home, a proviso granted to him when he was headhunted by a rival company a couple of years ago (just around the time that he broke into the top hundred of the Index, in fact, but let's not worry ourselves with the maths).

The important thing is that when it comes to writing ad slogans, the happiest person in the world is a genius. When he submits a slogan, his boss invariably tells him it is 'genius'. He does not believe that his boss actually considers him to be a genius, so he still values this frequent praise. Yet he himself knows, without any shadow of a doubt, that he is a genius. He's not arrogant about this. In fact, he keeps this knowledge to himself. Yet he doesn't kid himself about how little effort he actually puts into his well-paid job.

You'll know some of his slogans. He wrote the famous one about the chocolate bar, the witty one about the fast-food chain, the simple but brilliant one credited with reversing the fortunes of a crisis-hit High Street bank. And, you'd never guess, but all of his very best slogans, he thought them up within a matter of minutes, even seconds. His employers do not know this, neither do his colleagues, his friends, nor even his wife.

Yes, he's married. For the second time. It might surprise you that he's a divorcee but this is significant because he has something to compare this marriage to. He understands exactly how good this current relationship is.

His wife shares many, but not all, of his interests and opinions. They still have the occasional heated disagreement, followed by sensational make-up sex.

She is a professional too, earning a good wage – but marginally less than his own. Which is perfect because even this bloke possesses a modicum of male pride.

Significantly, she travels with her job – the exact nature of her employment is unimportant as she doesn't bring work home with her – but she is away from home for around two nights a week. This means the couple never seem to get bored of one other. In fact, he can't wait to see her, every time she returns from a trip. And he isn't bothered about the prospect of his wife copping off with a stranger she might meet in some foreign hotel bar. Partly because of a mild sexual perversion, which would mean that he would be turned on by such a liaison, as long his wife told him about it, which she would. And partly because he is as certain as he possibly can be that she is utterly devoted and faithful to him.

Of course, if his wife knew quite how little time her husband actually spent working, this would cause a certain resentment within their relationship (enough to relegate him from the world's top hundred, by some margin).

This is one of the very few secrets he holds from her and there is little likelihood of her ever finding it out. She would never suspect that a man so well-respected by his peers and so highly-paid by his company, could ever put in so few man hours. In this day and age of cost-cutting and austerity, that sort of thing just doesn't happen. At least, that's the generally-held perception.

Both the happiest person in the world and his wife have children from their previous marriages. Ironically, the right-wing British government which introduced the original Happiness Index would have imagined them to be thoroughly miserable (and immoral) solely by virtue of this fact.

He has one nine-year-old daughter and one seven-year-old son. The girl is academically gifted, has inherited his flair for words, but is also uncommonly sweet-natured. The boy is handsome, boisterous and sporty. Just the sort of son he had hoped for.

The happiest person on the planet sees his children two or three times a week. Again, this means he does not often truly miss them but is never bored nor irritated by them either. He almost always gets an excellent night's sleep and does not have to worry with the more troublesome aspects of parenthood. In fact he doesn't even know what these aspects are. His ex-wife, incidentally, has never featured in the top billion and is never likely to. There are tens of thousands of women in Haiti, Ethiopia and Yemen, for instance, who rank significantly higher than her.

So having just the right level of independence from his wife and kids, our man is perfectly disposed to benefit from the fact that one of the best real-ale pubs in England is a seven-minute walk away from his house. Not so close that he would ever have a quiet night in disturbed by the occasional rowdy punter. Yet near enough that inclement weather would never dissuade him from taking a stroll there.

So, having heard *Taco Wagon* five times and *This One's For The Ladies* once in its entirety, he is ready for a lunchtime visit to The Contented Pig, with its seven regular ales, plus two frequently-changing guests, all kept immaculately by the dry-witted landlord, beneath his original Tudor beams and beside the roaring flames of his inglenook fireplace.

It is Wednesday. His wife is due home this evening, after two nights away, and she has just sent him a filthy text message. Which only increases his thirst for a pint of Timothy Taylor Landlord, as he leaves his house, whistling *Taco Wagon*.

You're probably thinking that if you met this bloke, you'd find him insufferably smug, but you'd be wrong. While he certainly knows that he is happier than he's ever been, he has absolutely no idea that there are not several people living on the same street who are every bit as happy. Besides, he couldn't care less about keeping up with the Joneses, nor anybody else.

So when he enters The Contented Pig, our man is greeted heartily by a couple of familiar fellow drinkers as well as the barmaid, who guesses, correctly that he'd like a pint of Landlord. She is attractive but not beautiful, showing cleavage but not too much, almost imperceptibly flirtatious, in short everything that he would want from a barmaid. After all, luckily for him, he's only moderately good looking, and, therefore, of the relatively small number of women he ever meets, very few ever attempt to seduce him.

After a brief conversation with a fellow regular about football (he follows the sport enough for a pub chat, but does not endure the misery of actively supporting a team), he sinks into a comfy seat in the corner and has the brilliant idea of sending a text message to a friendly acquaintance who is a writer with Hollywood connections.

His text reads: "The next time you see Tarantino, you MUST tell him to use a track called *Taco Wagon* by the Young Fresh Fellows in his next movie. It would be perfect for him and it's properly obscure so would have just the sort of impact he loves from a soundtrack."

For while our man doesn't really know any famous people (famous people, as a rule, tending to make others miserable), he does always seem to know someone who knows someone famous.

The writer texts back shortly afterwards: "Just at airport off to LA and seeing Quentin at weekend! Will keep a note of it. No need to listen first, mate, know your taste is impeccable. Speak soon."

They wouldn't speak soon. But as he sups on his Landlord in The Contented Pig, the happiest person in the world is filled with warmth, knowing that he may have repaid the Young Fresh Fellows for all the pleasure they had given him down the years, thanks to a chance text message which would, in all likelihood, bring the band more money and fame than they had ever enjoyed in a quarter of century of making music in Seattle, both before, during and well after the time when Seattle was the centre of the musical universe.

However much the Index uses factors such as

gender, age, wealth and occupation to measure happiness, there is still much to be said in favour of performing a good deed for the day. And our man genuinely likes to do so.

Ascending to the bar, he thinks he receives a blink-and-you'd-miss-it wink from the barmaid, but he is uncertain of this.

"Same again, Swede Art," he says, in faux Cockney. The barmaid is Swedish and he thinks of her as a work of art but he is not conceited enough to explain to her such a decidedly average pun (he certainly would not submit it as an ad slogan).

"'Ere," calls a friendly face from the opposite side of the bar, "come and have a butcher's at this."

His fellow drinker has a laptop computer perched on the bar-top.

"I'm working from home," he chuckles, giving the inverted commas gesture.

"Me too," smiles our man.

"This is the funniest thing I've ever seen. You gotta love YouTube, eh?"

In fact, despite his media industry connections, the happiest person in the world has such a fulfilling life and such a high boredom threshold that he spends very little time online and is only barely aware of YouTube, yet he nods politely all the same.

As his companion clicks and fumbles and Googles away, he says: "You've got to remember this clip. You know when you're having a bad day at the office or the wife's nagging you or you're just feeling down with life ..."

The drinker pauses, and the happiest person in the world is suddenly struck by the realisation that he has not experienced any of those things for a couple of years at least. For a fleeting second, this troubles him greatly. Had somebody told him that there was, in fact, a Worldwide Happiness Index, he'd suddenly fancy himself to be right up there in the top 1%, perhaps even the top 0.1%. There is an uncomfortable realisation that the only way from here must be down. But as we have said, the feeling is fleeting. The man with the laptop isn't going to take all night locating his YouTube clip, now is he?

As the drinker tilts the screen around, the happiest person in the world sees the credits to The Sooty Show, then hears the voice of Matthew Corbett, over an image of a sleeping Sweep the Dog.

"He's actually dreaming that he is appearing on *Stars In Their Eyes*," says Corbett, "Sweep is dreaming that he is impersonating the famous opera singer, Luciano Pavarotti."

As Sweep appears, dressed in a white bow tie and tuxedo, our man lets out a giggle. As Sweep squeaks in his tuneless, wordless way to the strains of Nessun Dorma, the happiest person in the world begins to laugh uncontrollably. And as Sweep reaches a high-pitched crescendo, our man's ribs begin to tighten to such an extent that he is unable to breathe.

As the little dog takes his bow, before a standing ovation, the happiest person in the world collapses, purple-faced, from his bar stall, cracking his head on the floor, never to regain consciousness.

Going out, as all of us would wish to do, right at the very top.

2

MR KNOW IT ALL

I know. I can tell stuff. It's definitely not clairvoyance, because I can't see into the future. It's not mind-reading either because I know things about you that you don't even know yourself, yet. I just know. I don't mean to sound creepy. And I'm certainly not being boastful. Believe me, if you've lived with this all of your life, you wouldn't like it and you wouldn't crow about it. It makes you feel lonely a lot of the time. Because you can't really confide in the people you know and love. They'll just think you are a freak, a liar, a mentalist or all three.

Even in this London Underground carriage, half-empty out in the suburbs in the middle of the afternoon, I can tell a lot. The married couple opposite me appear to be very much in love, and indeed they are. But the wife is having an affair. An affair she actually doesn't even want to be having, but from which she cannot escape. Some sort of blackmail, emotional or otherwise. I don't know whether her husband will ever find out. I don't do the future, as I said. You wouldn't be able to detect her infidelity. She is holding her husband's hand and resting her head on his shoulder. Her affection for him isn't fake. The guilt is crippling her, yet nobody else would spot anything perceptible. She doesn't look guilty or sad or edgy. Her husband is unlikely to ever guess what she's up to, unless he's presented with some glaring evidence or eventuality. She's really rather good at hiding it all. I hope she manages to sort this all out. I don't feel judgmental at all. When you know as many things about as many people as I do, you really don't tend to judge. None of us are entirely good. In fact, not many of us are even close to being good, as far as I can tell.

The man to my left, the other side of a single empty seat, the poor bloke's got cancer. Prostate. He isn't aware of it yet. He appears healthy and does not have the haunted expression of a man who knows he is seriously ill. His wife, or perhaps his partner – he is not wearing a wedding ring, and there are occasional gaps in my knowledge, unless I really concentrate hard – she suspects something is not quite right with him but she doesn't want to nag him to go to the doctor. She really ought to. She's not here, not with him, but I know that she's worried about him. I wish I could tell him but I can't. What sort of lunatic goes up to a total stranger in a tube carriage and tells him he has cancer. See what I mean? Not an easy thing to live with, is it?

It's not all bad, though. I know that the attractive girl at the far end of the carriage has an intense craving to be handcuffed and dominated sexually. She's never done it, yet. She's only twenty-one and hasn't plucked up the courage to tell either of the boys she's slept with so far. You can't help but be either amused or aroused by that sort of knowledge. This, of course, is the kind of information you could use to your advantage and, as a younger man, I did. But when it comes to effectively cheating women into bed, the novelty wears off, to some extent. With women, with relationships, this absolute knowledge is more of a hindrance than a help.

Women like to think that they are more intuitive

than men, and perhaps they are as a rule, I really wouldn't know. So when it becomes obvious that you understand them completely, that you comprehend their every mood swing, this tends to irritate them. They like to be irrational, mysterious, enigmatic. When they feel that they can't be, you simply become a source of fury. Maybe you could pretend that you don't understand them, reverse psychology, but then it becomes obvious that you're a phony and the mind games escalate and the whole thing soon becomes pretty unworkable.

Then there are the more selfish aspects. I am told, and I can imagine, that those 'getting to know you' conversations at the start of relationships are one of life's great pleasures. Yet when you already know everything about everyone you meet, you end up hoping the woman will tell you lies just to give the situation a little intrigue. Women start to seem either tedious or devious. Of course, once they reach their 20s, they always lie about their number of sexual partners. You forgive them that. And at the start of a relationship, they tend to lie to you that they're not needy, about how easygoing they are when it comes to your drinking, your smoking, the amount of time they expect you to spend with them, the amount of time you spend with your mates, or going to gigs or football matches or whatever it is you like to do.

Personally I love films and novels. Fictional characters are the only people who can surprise me. I love to see how they develop, how they reveal themselves. I have to wait for the screenwriter or the author to tell me. It's magical. Had I met the writer, however, I'd imagine that I would know exactly what was going to happen in their film or book. It's always autobiographical to some extent, fiction, isn't it?

Women, though, in those early stages, they'll always lie about the same things. They'll lie that they find it endearing if you are untidy around the house or that you lack concern for your own appearance. But then again, even you must have realised they were lying about that by now. It's just that I always know all of this, even right at the start, even during the bit when you are blinded by lust, or even love. And that, of course, is the crux of it. You can't fall in love with a woman completely when you know everything about her. You might imagine that you and your lover have given yourselves entirely to one another but you never can. You must always maintain a little something for yourself. You wouldn't want to know all of each other's bitterness, hatreds, jealousies. But I know it all, and I wish that I didn't.

Okay, so you're probably now imagining that I'm full of shit, that I'm actually making all of this up. Well, regard the lady a few seats to my right. In her early 60s, but dressed a little younger. She has been married for 40 years but she only loves her dog. And this morning, her dog has run away. Yes, you can see for yourself that she is looking anxious, that she cannot wait for this tube train to emerge overground, as it will before the next station. But I can tell you that the reason for her anxiety is her lost dog. She is expecting a phone call from her recently-retired husband, who has had to cut short an afternoon in the pub to go hunting for the mongrel. Here we go, light at the end of the tunnel, up the slope, daylight, bingo, she's listening to a voicemail already. She's going to ring her husband.

"Still no sign? ... where have you looked? ... you've been round the park? ... oh God, we'll have to put up some signs, offer a reward, I can't believe this. If we get him back, I'll never leave him alone with you again.

I knew I shouldn't have but I had to visit Mum. They should allow dogs in the hospital, anyway, I can't understand it."

The wife of the couple opposite me is checking her phone, surreptitiously. There's no text message from her illicit lover. There never is, when he knows she is with her husband.

The man with prostate cancer has stood up and is moving from one foot to another as though he needs the toilet. He can't understand why. He went just before he got on the train but just recently he has been pissing like a racehorse.

And when I shoot this narrow-eyed look of intense seriousness directly into the eyes of the attractive 21-year-old girl at the end of the carriage, it almost seems to take her breath away. Did you notice that? I'm not a vain man, I know I'm a little out-of-shape and at the age of 32, a little too old for her. But if I just curl up my lip, almost imperceptibly at her. The suggestion of casual cruelty. Did you see what it did to her? Oh, baby ...

Anyway, I'll have to avert my gaze now. I'm off to see Jenny. I know my boss has sneaked off for a family event and that he won't trouble me for the rest of the day, so I don't even have to pretend to be 'working from home'. I haven't used my knowledge as well as I could have done in terms of my career path. I could have been an absolute star as a professional gambler. I can't predict the results of sporting events, exactly. But I could tell you if the centre-forward is nursing an injury or a secret heartache, for instance. Stocks and shares, speculating and accumulating, figures and finances, those sort of things leave me cold, so I have never really tried, but I reckon I could make a killing in that game. Anyway, I've done well enough for myself as it is, I'm able to base myself at home and I earn more money than I need.

The strange thing is, I'm going to see Jenny and I'm going to tell her. Tell her everything. I've never told a girlfriend everything before. I don't know whether Jenny is special, exactly, and I still assume there's a fair chance that telling her is going to freak her out and make her ditch me. I just feel the need to tell somebody, just to see whether it might work for me. I've never told anybody all of it before. I've hinted at it, gone round the houses, but that's only made me sound even weirder. I've lost one good friend and distanced myself from another, by being partial with the truth. And the whole truth seems to be an intolerable burden at times. I like Jenny, though. She's never told me any filthy black lies, which I appreciate. A few half-truths and white lies but nothing that you would ever have guessed. She really is one of the most honest and decent people I've ever met. I'm reckoning that maybe she might just believe me and that she might not finish with me. The way she makes me feel, I reckon she might even be able to help me cope with it all better.

Despite knowing far too much about everyone I meet, I crave friendship and togetherness, more than most. I guess this is because, as a young child, I was a weirdo. For obvious reasons, given all of this. These days the child psychologists would have labelled me autistic or something. I have no respect for psychiatrists. They know so little about what they profess to be experts in. They're bullshit artists, from what I can make out, even the better ones. You'd be better off going to see an astrologist or a tarot-card reader, really you would. You'd certainly be better off making an appointment to sit on my couch, had I decided to go into that line of business. I wouldn't need any degree or diploma. And yet there is a difference between knowing and caring. I might know everything about everyone but I am rarely all that bothered.

When I got old enough to understand what was so different about me, I was able to disguise it. Then I became particularly good at making friends. I understood that some people who appeared friendly towards me, actually couldn't stand me and that other more diffident kids were really rather fond of me. The friends I made found me remarkably understanding, which, of course, I was. I understood everything about them.

It has never been easy, though, with my parents. They obviously knew there was something strange about me from early childhood and yet they never took the time to discover exactly what. At that stage I couldn't articulate it, anyway. By the time I reached my teens, I simply wasn't inclined to explain it to them, especially as I knew everything about their marriage – and who on earth would want to know the intimate details of their own parents' marriage? In short, I knew that my mother hated sex and that my father slept around, and I knew this before I had ever felt lust or any of the other adult feelings which would have allowed me to understand. So as I entered puberty, I began to pity my mum and dad. There are plenty of feelings a teenager should have towards their parents – embarrassment, irritation, anger, sullen indifference – but genuinely pitying them was just plain odd.

* * * * *

I am more optimistic than I should have any right to be as I alight the tube station at the penultimate stop, almost through the suburbs and out into the actual sticks. Jenny lives a ten-minute walk from the station. She works from home, too. She's an artist. Water colours mainly. I admire her work but she is self-conscious about it. She doesn't like to talk about it too much. I've never been allowed to see one of her paintings before she has completed it, either. Most men who've known Jenny, who've loved or lusted after her, would feel jealous or irritated by this. They would feel as though they were being excluded, not being fully trusted, by her refusing them access to her mind's inner sanctum. I respect this, though, I understand that she needs complete privacy to allow her creativity to blossom.

She knows I'm coming over. It's unusual for me to head round to hers in the afternoon but she's easygoing about it. She says she's bought in some wine and doughnuts and ice cream. She wants to treat herself a little. It'll be a relaxed atmosphere, I can feel it, and although there's part of me that doesn't want to disturb this serenity, I know there may never be a better chance than this to tell her what I need to tell her. We've been seeing each other for three months now, maybe only a couple of times a week, and we only slept together for the first time two weeks ago. She seems remarkably easy to be with, there's not a hint of neediness about her. She's the first woman I've ever known who I've really felt the need to tell.

Jenny answers the door in a white bathrobe, the kind she might have stolen from an expensive hotel. She has long, red hair and a lightly freckled face. When she is naked, though, the acute pallor and softness of her skin reminds you of virgin snow. Sometimes you don't even want to touch her, just admire her. We kiss and she leads me by my hand into the lounge. There's a bottle of dry white wine in an ice bucket on her coffee table. Art books scattered around it, scattered everywhere. Jenny's own works on the walls, among others. She likes you to guess which paintings are hers and which are not. I know, of course, and she seems impressed, amazed even, when I've 'guessed' correctly nine times out of ten. The tenth time I've deliberately got it wrong, just so she doesn't think I'm some sort of stalker or guess that I'm whatever the hell I am. That I'm Mr fucking Know It All.

We sip wine, we hold hands, I stroke at her breasts inside her robe but I don't feel like making love and I don't want to drink too much wine in the afternoon. I need to tell her now. Tell her here. Not drunkenly, not post-coitally. Now. I have to take the leap.

"Jen, I really like you a lot, and there's something I really need to tell you."

My left hand is gently clasping the back of her neck and my right hand is rubbing at her thigh. I'm looking straight into her eyes but suddenly I cannot tell what Jenny is feeling. I am struck by the realisation that I know a hundred times more about the insignificant woman on the tube train who'd lost her dog than I do about the woman right before me, the woman I might very well love. Like a black hole in the airwaves, right at the very frequency of your favourite radio station. Nothing there but a low buzz of interference. Jenny doesn't appear worried or intrigued or even concerned by what I have said. This is not what I had envisaged. I feel as if I am walking over a cliff. I feel like any one of you would feel in a similar situation. It's uncomfortable for me, though, entirely unfamiliar. This mild air of panic. This must be how uncertainty feels.

Jenny moves away and fixes my gaze.

"Did you hear what I said?" I ask.

"Yes, Mark, I heard you. But you have to keep calm and listen to me. It's time I told you something about me first."

I am, it's fair to say, not easily caught off-guard or wrong-footed. There were no terrifying skeletons in this woman's closet. So why this need to take control of the conversation, just as I had clearly been about to tell her something of rare significance?

She holds my hand.

"I know about you. I know about your knowledge. Your gift," she says.

I am hit by a sudden blast of refrigerated air. "You know?"

"I know you have a rare gift. I know you know an awful lot about people. I don't think you know quite as much as you may think you do but you instinctively know an incredible amount."

"How? How do you know? And what do you mean 'I don't know as much as I think I know'?"

I had expected her to react with shock, awe, incredulity, fear. Not to respond with a casual act of one-upmanship.

"You don't know about me, do you?"

"I know a lot about you, Jen. I know a lot about everyone. Pretty much everything, I think."

"Babe, you don't know that I'm not an artist. At least, I don't make my living from it."

"These paintings aren't yours?"

"Some of them are, babe, one or two, but it's only a hobby, I'm not good enough to be a professional. The artist thing, I'm afraid, it's a cover story."

A cover story? This is impossible to me. I just don't get caught off guard like this. I remember a jackdaw flying into my lounge once. Have you ever had a bird fly into your house? That's how this makes me feel. That's the only metaphor I have. Nothing else has ever happened to me that was quite so unexpected. It kept crashing into the walls, this jackdaw. Crashing around and shitting on the carpet. They are big old birds. Big when they're in a small room. Evil looking. They don't think much, birds. I rarely understand much about any animals, even if I really focus on them. Those who choose vegetarianism on the basis that animals are sentient beings, really don't have that much of a case. You wouldn't like animals if you knew them. They really aren't all that sentient at all in my experience. They are thick and entirely self-obsessed, as a rule. Especially birds. The budgie we had as a child, Christ it was every bit as boring as you could have imagined. 'Where's my trill, where's my cuttlefish, where's my mirror? There it is! Oh, who's a pretty boy? I'm a pretty fucking boy'. Self-obsessed, like I say.

Jenny shifts uncomfortably on the sofa, having released this conversational jackdaw into my living space. Why would she need a 'cover story'? I look at her, I concentrate on her in a way that I rarely need to do. And usually if I concentrate really hard, I can tell what it is that I need to know, what I want to know, about someone on those rare occasions when there is something that is not instinctively obvious to me. But with Jenny now, there is nothing there, nothing registering. Is this how it feels to the rest of you, so much of the time? I used to envy you all, but now I am not so sure. Now I think I prefer things the way they always used to be.

"You were going to tell me something about yourself, Jen, something which sounded as if it was going to be significant and then you said something about a cover story. Jen, what the fuck are you going on about? Because I really don't know and that scares me because, as I think you know, I know a lot, I thought I knew it all, pretty much, until just now."

Her eyes are darting around at her paintings. Not HER paintings, it seems. The paintings in her lounge. Her cover story. I want to put my foot or my fist through each and every canvas. Jenny is strikingly beautiful, though, at this moment, more so than most.

"I work for the Government," she says.

The walls seem closer together now. I need to breathe some fresh air. I undo an extra shirt button, then unbutton my cuffs too.

"What do you mean the Government? MI5 or something?"

"No, no. Not MI5. People think MI5 is so impressive. Everyone knows about MI5. They're just civil servants, paper pushers. They're muggles, you know, we call them muggles, like in Harry Potter."

"Muggles are the ones who aren't wizards, right?"

"Yeah that's right."

"So you're a fucking wizard are you, Jen?"

"We're both not a million miles away from wizards, Mark. We're categorised as supernatural, psychologically and emotionally supernatural, that's the accepted term for us."

"I don't think I've been categorised before. Are we a category? Are there many of us? I mean, are you the same as me or something?"

"I'm similar, really quite similar. I'm trained though. You haven't been trained, yet."

"Yet?"

"I was detailed to recruit you."

"Did they detail you to fuck me too?"

The skin on Jen's face reddens. 'They' obviously

haven't trained her to avoid blushing.

"I wasn't supposed to make love with you, no. That wasn't supposed to have happened, I'm sorry."

"Right so you're a bit of a shit wizard then aren't you? Not exactly supernatural at all. Or is a piece of cock like Kryptonite to you or something?"

I fasten my shirt buttons and put on my shoes but she grabs at my wrist.

"You can't go."

"Why not? Are there secret service men surrounding the house? Out in the bushes or somewhere? Is there a Government helicopter over-head? Are you recording this conversation? Am I being bugged?"

"No. None of that. At least, I don't think so. Listen."

"I don't want to fucking listen."

"It's a shock for you babe, I know, you're not in control and you've always been in control. Always had so much knowledge. I know it feels strange when that's been taken away from you but please hear me out. I have ice cream and doughnuts in the fridge."

"I don't feel hungry, Jen. I don't understand and I don't want to understand. I want to leave now and I want to go back to my life, which is actually quite an ordinary life, on the face of it at least, and you can go back to your superhero life and you can save the world on behalf of the Government or whatever it is that you do and we can pretend this whole thing never happened, ok?"

"No, no that's not ok. First of all, as I said, we weren't supposed to – I wasn't supposed to – sleep with you."

"Oh so you're just worried you'll be in trouble? You think I'm going to grass you up to Dumbledore or Zeus or whoever it is you work for?"

"No. And stop taking the piss. I've had enough of you taking the piss."

The tone of her voice has changed. I like this. It's as if she has almost lost control. Suddenly, she's just a fiery redhead on the verge of a temper tantrum, rather than some crack government agent with superpowers that trump my own. She doesn't sound so superior now. And so I sit back on the sofa and think I might as well listen to what she has to say. Ignore it but listen to it first, at least.

"Okay, I'll listen then."

"Okay, thank you. I mean it, thank you for listening. I know it's a shock and I know what it feels like to be shocked when you're not used to ever being shocked, in this manner at least. It's like when that jackdaw flew into your house that time."

"I've never told you that ... fuck, you're good."

Jen smiled, an uncomfortable smile but at least it was good to know you could still successfully flatter her.

"You're good too, babe, you really are extraordinary, more so than I was when they recruited me, I reckon. It's just that they have taught me some techniques, to deflect you from me, to deflect other gifted people from knowing me. Foreign governments use people like us too. And they work, these techniques, to some extent, but we all have our weaknesses."

"Cock?"

"I'm more of an eyes girl, to be honest."

"Eyes?"

"You have amazing eyes."

"I bet you say that to all the superheroes."

"I'm relatively new to all this. I have only been working for them for two years."

She is business-like again. She tightens the toweling belt on her robe.

"Anyway, listen. First the spiel. Their spiel. There are very few of us in the UK. As far as we know, fewer than fifty. There may be more but probably not many more. Since the unit was set up, it's unlikely now that there are too many of us out there who are unknown to the unit."

"Unit? That sounds a bit shit. Can't we be a coven or something more magical-sounding?"

"Just try and stop being flippant, babe, just for a while. Around 20 of us are full-time employees, most of the rest work for the unit on an ad hoc basis, that is their choice. It'll be your choice too. A few are very reluctant but are basically onside. There have only been a couple who have been hostile about the whole thing and frankly – between you and me – I wouldn't advise you to go down that route."

"Is that some sort of a threat?"

"No it's an honest assessment from someone who has come to care about you. The pay and conditions are outstanding because, as you can imagine, they can't exactly advertise these roles in the job centre."

"Pension schemes and private health care and six-figure salaries for wizards?"

"Can you forget the wizard thing? It's unhelpful. We're not wizards as such, you know what we are, we're gifted that's all."

"Ok, no more wizards."

"If you wish to come on board, full-time or part-time, they will train you well. The whole process, in many ways, makes life easier to deal with because it isn't easy is it, dealing with this? Quite lonely, you know what I mean?"

"Of course I know what you mean and I know that

you know that I know what you mean, that's how this works."

"So those are the benefits and the spiel is basically this: there are a lot of bad people out there who want to kill us and maim us and take away our freedoms and threaten our way or life in all manner of ways. How do you imagine that so few terrorists ever succeed? Terrorism is easy. If you're a suicidal fanatic it is the easiest thing in the world to get hold of explosives and blow people sky high."

"Well, there's intelligence ..."

"Yes, but normal intelligence isn't enough. Muggles aren't enough. They need our sort of intelligence. At least that's the spiel."

"You keep saying 'that's the spiel' as if you're not convinced about it all?"

"I need to go outside for a cigarette," she says and puts her finger to her lips. Jen is a non-smoker.

She slips on her slippers, stands up and beckons me out through the kitchen into the garden.

I have never been into her garden before. The flower beds are beautifully maintained, there is a large apple tree in the centre of the lawn and its white blossom dances around the grass in the light breeze.

She puts her hands on my hips, not knowing whether I will flinch, but I don't. She rubs her hand against my lower spine. This feels right, despite everything, somehow.

"I'm convinced about it all in theory," she says, "I was convinced when they approached me. I felt it was my absolute duty to come on board, to join the unit – and I know I've done a lot of good. I know I can do a lot more too."

"But? What's the 'but' – apart from the fact that you do obviously think your spooks have been bugging us back there in the lounge?"

"I don't think so but I don't know for sure. We don't know it all do we? We know about people. We know about their lives, their feelings, their relationships, their fears, all of that, but we don't know the answers to every general knowledge question, we don't know how to fix a washing machine, we certainly don't know how to detect bugging devices. There are muggles who are, to some extent, in control of the unit. The head of the unit is one of us but he has to report to a muggle. The politicians don't know about us at all, the Prime Minister even. None of them. Because the top brass want to take all the credit for what amazing 'intelligence' they have, when, in fact, employing people like us is such a huge advantage that it's basically cheating. So to me the 'but' is that foiling terrorism and maintaining national security isn't everything is it? I mean, what about those cancer moments? You saw a man on the Tube coming over here. You see someone who has cancer but they don't know it and it may be curable now but perhaps not when it's finally diagnosed. Or when you see someone heartbroken and you know they could so easily mend it? I think I'd rather help people than help the Government."

"But you're in the system now, they won't let you out of it, will they?"

"The way I see it is that they've brought us all together now, we are not just one or two crackpots or freaks. I've met a lot of us and most of us are really good, seemingly normal people, which is heartening to know. We haven't used our 'gifts' for criminal ends or to con people or control them in some sinister way. We're all just pretty lonely, a little fucked-up for obvious reasons, but we're good people, Mark."

"I used to trick women into bed with it – with the gift or whatever you call it."

Jen smiles.

"Of course you did, you're a bloke, it's the first thing any bloke would do. Oh, and by the way, about 90 per cent of us are women. I think you're one of only six men that we're aware of. But anyway you didn't need to trick women into bed, did you? We're here, aren't we? Talking like this. You didn't trick me."

I smile. Sunlight cuts a swathe through the clouds, illuminating an English suburban garden. Gloating birds chirp songs of self-praise. 'Look at me, I'm sitting in a tree, I can sit in whichever fucking tree I like. I'm a pretty boy.'

"I guess so. I still don't quite understand what you're saying, though. What it is that you want to do. This is all quite a lot to take in, Jen. I was coming here to tell you I had the most extraordinary gift in the world – and I'd never really told anyone properly about it before – so it was going to be a pretty big deal. Then I find out I'm just one of many and you're one of many. And now this."

"I know, baby, I know but we have strength in numbers now. We're together and we're better than them, better than the muggles. They're just fighting a war. They're the good guys, of course, but they're warriors all the same. Maybe they are bugging us, I don't know, but they're emotionally retarded, compared to us, and that's what matters."

"You must have a good gardener, it's immaculate out here."

"No, I garden. I paint. I bake. I don't think it's my calling to be a counter-terrorist. Even though I've done my bit already, I really have. But I could do a lot more, we all could. The way I see it is that what we need is a leak. We need the existence of the unit, the existence of all of us, to be leaked somehow. Then we'd be free to use what we have for the betterment of everyone, not just the Government."

And as she speaks like this, it becomes clear to me that those deflecting techniques have been forgotten and that Jen has laid out her soul to me. And she really is remarkably nice, at the core of her being, she is possibly the nicest person I have ever met. There is no side to her at all. Even after two years spent at the heart of some shadowy governmental counter-terrorism unit there isn't an ounce of cynicism present. She is an idealist who wants only to use her gift to make the world a better place. A radical idealist, willing to create a major storm inside, and possibly outside, of the secret services. As we stand beneath her apple tree it would not surprise me were she to suddenly start singing about honey bees and snow-white turtle doves. Yes, the realisation is crushing, but almost instantaneous. Jenny is fundamentally wet.

And me? Well, I am certain now that I just want a quiet life. I don't want to get involved in any of this. I don't want to be a counter-terrorist and I don't want to expose the existence of some supernatural unit either. In fact, I will never tell anybody about my gifts again. As a result of this, I may never know true love nor genuine intimacy, I may never save a man from cancer nor a woman from heartbreak but I understand that it will be infinitely preferable to simply keep myself to myself in the future.

Soon, I am going to make my excuses, leave Jen's place and leave Jen's life. I might try to track down that young girl I saw on my Tube journey over here. Yes, I'll find her in the bar where I know she often drinks. Get myself invited back to her place, to give her what she wants. It'd be easy, perhaps too easy, but I still reckon it'd be an awful lot of fun.

3

SIXTEEN

So there he was. A 39-year-old man in love with a girl of 15. Which is not quite as reprehensible, as seedy, or as illegal as it might sound. Yet still every bit as sad. The 15-year-old girl in question would be 38 herself by now, provided she wasn't dead. Which, he had begun to fear, was entirely possible.

It seemed difficult to imagine that one woman of 38 could be so entirely immune to the joys, or otherwise, of Friends Reunited, Facebook and Twitter. Or of having simply kept in touch with a single school friend through old-fashioned, conventional means. Yet when he came to think about it, if any woman could manage to stay completely off the social networking radar, it would have been Claire Davis. Or at least the 15-year-old girl Claire Davis had been and the sort of 38-year-old woman she'd have been most likely to become. Claire Davis with her bog-standard, ordinary, muck-common name, which made her so difficult to track down during late-night cyber-stalking sessions.

And, yes, he realised Claire would probably be married by now and would, despite the defiant air of independence she'd always possessed, quite possibly have a different surname these days. But there was nobody on Facebook called Claire with a single mutual friend who could have fitted the bill. He'd checked every friend of every school friend. Then re-checked at regular intervals. Not that Claire Davis had had many school mates. He wasn't sure if he could recall her having one genuine friend, other than himself. She had been far more of an outcast than he. In fact, despite having been one of the brightest students, academically, at a school in which intelligence was often treated like leprosy, he hadn't really been an outcast at all.

After leaving school, he had only really bothered to stay in touch with his best friend, Max, yet he had emailed several old school-mates on Friends Reunited and made Facebook friends with several more. Not through any genuine concern as to their well-being or whereabouts. Had he cared enough, he would have kept in contact in the first place. No, he was always hinting, always fishing, occasionally even simply asking for any possible information as to the whereabouts of Claire Davis. There had been no clues, no leads, not even a vague idea that Claire had gone to this university or headed down that career path. Nobody had the slightest idea and nobody else seemed to care.

When a school reunion had been staged a couple of years earlier, he had attended by virtue of the slimmest of hopes that Claire Davis had been silently monitoring her former school-mates online for all of this time, without ever making herself visible, and that she would appear, perhaps with the intention of seeing him, perhaps just on some curious whim. Yet, of course, she didn't. And, equally predictably, the evening had turned out to be a depressing experience. Men indulging in metaphorical cock-waving about their salaries, women surreptitiously trying to out-do each other as to who had the busiest life. Working mums versus stay-at-home mums versus childless career women. Busyness was next to Godliness. Had Claire Davis been there, he felt sure she would have made a point of exaggerating how relaxed and stress-free her life was, even if it wasn't stress-free or relaxed at all. She'd always gone out of her way never to have been 'one of the girls'.

Still, it was now a decade since he'd discovered Friends Reunited; six years since he'd joined Facebook and three years since he'd opened a Twitter account and only now was he beginning to give up hope.

While he may have imagined many moments he thought that he'd shared with Claire during their school days, and while he'd certainly forgotten many more, there were only a few memories of her in which he was entirely confident. Despite this yearning which had nagged at him for well over half a lifetime, he was no hopeless romantic. He was well aware of how ridiculous his obsession was. And in his mind, the authenticity of only two or three little scenes between Claire Davis and he were undoubted.

The most significant was certainly this: on their final day at school, when he had just turned 16 and Claire Davis was approaching her own 16th birthday, he'd worn a white shirt which had been quickly covered with signatures and wishes of good luck from friends and other classmates. Most of the other kids had done likewise. Claire Davis, however, had taken the more mature or old-fashioned approach of bringing in an autograph book. Sitting together in their form room, as they had often done, Claire had passed him the book. He had flicked through the previous pages, there were a few scrawled names and meaningless platitudes from other classmates. He knew that he didn't want to merely scrawl his name in

Claire's autograph book. He knew he didn't want to write her a meaningless platitude. He knew for certain that Claire Davis regarded him with some degree of genuine fondness but, as for anything else, he knew nothing. All he knew at this moment was that he wanted Claire Davis to remember him. He wanted her to know that she meant something to him. She waited as he kneaded his forehead, pen poised for an inordinate amount of time. Sensing, perhaps, that her watching him was making him nervous, she turned away, went and spoke to somebody else, and did not return for a few minutes.

By which time he had scribbled this:

'My very best wishes for the future, Charlie Snell.'

"Oh," said Claire Davis, with a thin smile of disappointment, and in a casual tone of voice, "I thought you were going to write that you love me."

And Claire Davis definitely did say those words. Despite having never said anything remotely similar to him before. Despite 23 years having passed since. He remembered her saying those words with absolute clarity. And he was certain that she had been sincere, that she not been making fun of him, because that would not have been in her nature. And, in hindsight, he felt certain that she had wanted him to write, in her autograph book, that he loved her. After that scene, he had strongly suspected that she'd loved him too; had loved him for those previous couple of years, perhaps every bit as much as he had loved her.

Even having scribbled such a bland platitude in Claire's autograph book, he could have retrieved the situation by telling her that of course he loved her, that surely it must have been obvious. Despite the fact they'd only ever kissed in a play, as part of their GCSE drama course. Yet, instead, he opened and closed his mouth like some mentally-deficient goldfish before Claire Davis picked up her autograph book, smiled and turned away.

"Best wishes yourself, Charlie Snell," she'd told him.

* * * * *

He had hated his 16-year-old self for that scene ever since. His sweating pores, his throbbing pulse, his hog-tied tongue. How could he have frozen at that very moment? How could he have underestimated its lasting importance? How could he have been so agonisingly shy? Some hormonal, pubescent trip-switch had prevented him from expressing his feelings. It wasn't even as if he would remain such a social inadequate for long.

Within a year he would become a rather more cocksure A-level college student. Smoking cigarettes, drinking beer in the less officious pubs and losing his virginity to a cinema usherette called Donna Summers, known as Donna Summers-Not-Donna-Summer-Donna-Summers. They first fucked after she had finished a late-night shift at the Odeon. She had still been wearing the upper half of her uniform. Ever since then the smell of popcorn had given him an erection. Donna-Summers-Not-Donna-Summer-Donna-Summers hadn't made him feel like Claire Davis had done, though. They'd never shared that effortless empathy, that ability to tolerate a long silence and dispense with all the bullshit.

Neither had Maisy Driscoll, the hippy chick from university, his first long-term relationship. Nor Emma Gomez, with her intriguing easel and her siesta eyes. Nor Beverley Jones, the first girl he'd ever lived with and the first girl he'd ever grown truly bored of. Nor

Lisa Maybank, who'd demanded the enactment of a different sexual fantasy every night and was the only woman he'd ever known who could successfully orphan lust from any other emotion.

Most significantly, Penny Holloway didn't make Charlie Snell feel the way Claire Davis had made him feel. And Charlie was entirely aware that she didn't, even when he married her, weeks before his 30th birthday.

He knew he'd been fully aware of his own feelings in advance of the wedding, because he had distinctly remembered telling Max a week before the big day – in Max's flat, with its forensic tidiness, around about midnight, as they drank mugs of tea after a session in the pub.

Max had smiled as he'd asked Charlie the question, with the easy certainty of a man who thought he knew its inevitable answer.

"So no doubts about getting married then, mate? You know I love Pen but as best man, I suppose it's my duty to ask you."

At first Max simply thought that Charlie hadn't been listening to his question. They were both half-cut and a little sleepy, hence the tea.

"No doubts about the wedding, mate?" he'd asked, a touch louder, still smiling.

This time, Max realised that Charlie's silence was meaningful, not lazy. They were two Englishmen, both now wishing that they'd had drunk a couple of extra pints of beer to numb them for the uncomfortable conversation ahead.

"Fuck, Charlie, surely not?"

"Some doubts, I guess, to be totally honest."

"I'm sure it's natural to have some doubts. Must be. It's a huge step isn't it? Taking the plunge. I can't imagine doing it, not yet. Not found the right woman, like you have though, mate."

"Like I said, I'm not sure. I'm not sure she is the right woman. You know, she's bright and caring and beautiful and sexy – and financially solvent! – and all my family love her, you love her. And I, um ..."

Max didn't know what to do with the silence he'd just been invited to fill.

"So what's the problem?"

"I don't think I'm in love with her."

"Yeah but there's love and there's 'in love'. Doesn't 'in love' only last a certain amount of time? You've been together, what, four years?"

"Yeah but I was never in love with Penny. Things just happened, we moved in together because we were already virtually living together, she started talking about marriage and kids, then her sister got married and got pregnant and it just sort of seemed to be what you did next."

"I'm sure this is all just pre-wedding nerves mate. Who's to say what being 'in love' means anyway? How do you define these things?"

"I know what being in love is, mate."

"Who've you been in love with then? Dozy Maisy from uni? That Spanish artist bird? Definitely not Beverley. Surely not Donna-Summers-not-Donna-Summer-Donna-Summers?"

"Claire Davis."

"Claire Davis at school? What? Have you kept in touch or something?"

"Nope. She's not even on Friends Reunited or anything. Never heard from her since the day I left school - but I've thought about her pretty much every single day since."

"But that's ridiculous. You were a kid. A Child."

"I know it's ridiculous, Max, but it also happens to be absolutely fucking true."

It was the first and last time he'd ever mentioned his feelings for Claire Davis to anybody – and Max really wasn't the right person to have confided in.

"Shit. I wish I hadn't asked. Though I know I should have asked. Shit."

"Don't tell Nicola."

"Of course I won't tell Nicola. She's just bought a hat for the wedding. It makes her look a proper twat."

They laughed, both knowing that Max and Nicola wouldn't last long.

"What are you going to do?" asked Max.

"I guess I'm going to have to get married. When else is Nicola going to wear her hat? You hate horse-racing. When else does a girl get to wear a twattish hat?"

"You have to want to marry her – but Penny is lovely, mate, she's a diamond."

"I know. And worse things happen. Worse things happen at sea."

"Piracy."

"Death by drowning."

"That Mike Oldfield tune."

"Lots of worse things happen at sea."

Max couldn't bear the meaningful nature of this conversation and so, with music being their shared, meaningless passion, Max started talking about the debut album by the Kings of Leon, which he'd recently bought. They swapped tea for whisky and listened to *Youth and Young Manhood*.

"You know you could have been a wonder, taking your circus to the sky ..."

Charlie loved the record, still believed the Kings of Leon had never topped it, and, somewhere along the way, he'd left his doubts on the shelf. Within three years, Penny had caught him cheating with a girl he more-or-less hated, and within four years, Charlie and Penny were divorced. Charlie had told Max he'd told him so, that night at the flat. Max shrugged shoulders. Charlie still had the wedding photos and Max had been right about one thing, Nicola looked like a twat in several of them.

Yet the one picture he'd possessed of Claire Davis, a fifth-form class photo – with Charlie sitting smirking in the centre of the front row and Claire looking diffident on the far left of the middle row – had been lost in the attic of the marital home. By his late 30s, Charlie was struggling to even create a faithful likeness of Claire's 15-year-old face in his mind. He doubted whether he'd recognise her if she walked past him in the street, even though he always looked out for her. He once wondered whether a woman on the London Underground had been Claire. He didn't think she was, but for the first time ever, he couldn't be quite certain that she wasn't. That same impossibly fair hair, that same ardent sadness in her expression. He was far bolder then than he'd been when he was sixteen. In fact, fellow commuters breathed sharply at the sheer devil-may-care approach of a man willing to talk to a (probable) stranger on the Tube.

"Excuse me, you're not Claire Davis are you?"

"No, no, sorry, I'm not," answered the stunned woman, in a Scottish accent.

"Sorry, just someone I went to school with and you look like her, that's all."

"Oh, right, no, I'm sorry."

"I loved her, actually, at school, Claire Davis ..."

The Tube doors opened and the woman scuttled away. He didn't see her nervously waiting on the same platform for the next Tube, trying not to catch his eye. The man hanging on the strap beside Charlie shot him a look of pure hatred. Charlie alighted, unnecessarily, at the next station, then guessed that the Scottish woman might see him when the following Tube came along and so he literally ran for the exit and the nearest pub. And that had been the only possible sighting of Claire Davis in almost a quarter of a century.

* * * * *

Despite this longing, Charlie had rarely been single for any length of time. During his marriage to Penny, he'd stumbled across Claudia - the unlovely woman he'd had an affair with - while searching for Claire Davis on Facebook. Then there was Bella, the rebound girl, who'd made him laugh, genuinely like no other female had ever done, but who was slovenly and ate cheese on toast in bed every night. Crumbs became embedded under his skin. A couple of very short-term flings and then Sally, who lasted a year, and who possessed an unerring confidence which women were never supposed to enjoy, at least not women you knew. Perhaps he'd never really got to know her. He was relieved when she dumped him, even though that break-up was only ever going to be HER decision.

Finally, now, there was Zoe, who was wondering, after nine months as his girlfriend, whether they might move in together or whether Charlie was just pathologically afraid of commitment. Zoe, who was sweet-natured and easy to be with. Zoe, who had grown to enjoy sharing his love of a country pub and a bracing walk. Zoe, who, despite her being several years his junior, he felt he could happily drift into middle-age with. If he had not already arrived in middle-age, as the country pubs and bracing walks seemed to suggest.

Yet Zoe wanted children – 'some time, no pressure, although it's not as if we're getting any younger' – and Charlie wasn't thinking of Claire Davis any less. In fact, whenever Zoe seemed to suggest their relationship move forward any further, he thought of Claire Davis all the more. He thought of his pathetic 16-year-old self and he found himself regressing into that 16-year-old self for longer and longer spells.

He'd been a 16-year-old virgin and like most 16-year-old virgins, he'd been convinced he was the only 16-year-old virgin in the world, or in his own school at least. He also doubted whether there were many 15-year-old virgins either. He was entirely convinced that Claire Davis was no virgin. This was due to a widespread rumour that she'd had inappropriate contact with a PE teacher – a rumour which had some semblance of truth. The teacher had been suspended. Charlie had remembered Claire punching a girl who had called her a slag. The accusing girl had been something of a slag herself, he seemed to recall. Claire had confided in him about the pain these rumours had caused her but he'd never dared asked her what the truth of it all had been.

When Claire Davis had hinted, with sledgehammer subtlety, that he might invite her to the school prom, he'd botched the job by blurting out that he'd presumed she'd be going with Mr Minton, the PE teacher. This was a memory even less palatable than his inability to sign Claire's autograph book with anything other than a forgettable cliche. Yet she hadn't seemed particularly angered by his unintentional insult, merely irritated by his crippling fear of making his affections known. As a result, neither of them had attended the school prom.

Zoe would have known how Claire Davis had felt. With her laidback nature and blissful lack of complications, she was more like Claire Davis than any woman Charlie had been with. She felt at home in Charlie's house, perhaps more at home than he'd have liked her to feel. She'd curl up on the sofa with a glass of wine and she was in love with his cat, Fido. It was when Charlie had told her he had a cat called Fido that he'd first made her laugh, on the night they'd met, through mutual friends. By the end of that night she was telling him how much she'd love to meet Fido. Fido had got him laid. Payback for all those early-morning lung-fulls of jellied pilchard fumes, the dead birds, the live mice and the Benny Hill-style chase routines which preceded Fido's capture before each visit to the cattery or vet.

There was never the slightest suggestion that Charlie Snell wasn't happy when sharing a sofa with Zoe and Fido. Yet there was always a nagging doubt, a distant dread, that she was about to try and say something meaningful. If she aimed a certain look into the distance, he would feign intense interest in the daftest of TV programmes, attempt to start zealous debates about any item in the news, anything to distract her. Until one night he was caught off guard. He'd been emptying the bin, was preoccupied with mundanity, when Zoe pounced.

"Charlie?" she asked, with undisguised significance in her voice.

"Yeah," he answered, with grim resignation in his own.

"Are we, you know, going anywhere?"

"Um, the Cotswolds next month for that weekend,

dinner at Max's next Friday ..."

"You know what I mean."

There was a silence. Fido started clawing, uncharacteristically, at Charlie's leg.

"Is our relationship going to progress anywhere, Charlie? I love being with you but I think I deserve to know. You know me, I'm not a nag, I never get at you."

"I know, I know you're not a nag."

"But you're not in love with me are you?"

Another silence. Fido was licking his own arsehole.

"I don't know, babe. I love being with you."

"But if you were in love with me, you'd know."

"I guess."

"What is it with you, Charlie? What is it you want?"

Charlie wanted Claire Davis. He wanted to scream that he wanted Claire Davis, only he never could. Because there was no Claire Davis. Not the Claire Davis he'd imagined she'd be. Perhaps no Claire Davis at all.

"Charlie, you obviously don't think it's even worth talking about, so I think I'm going to go home now."

"Sometimes, Zoe, sometimes I feel as though I'm still sixteen years old."

Most women would have been intrigued by such a line and would have seized upon it, hopefully, as a starting point for an in-depth, analytical discussion. But Zoe wasn't like most women. She wasn't intrigued by his whimsical self-pity. She didn't want to talk about the child inside the man. As she took to her feet, as she stroked and caressed Fido that last time, Charlie admired this trait in her. He realised he'd be uncommonly lucky to find another woman anything like her. He wanted to tell her this, at the very least, but somehow he couldn't quite find the words.

And so as Zoe left the house, he offered her, with quiet sincerity, his very best wishes for the future.

4

A MILD-MANNERED MAN

There are hailstones hammering against the patio doors of my ground-floor apartment. Such is the intense quiet of this place – even in the heart of a town, in the middle of a day, in the centre of a week – that I welcome the sound of the filthy weather. It's either that or the ticking of the clock, almost imperceptible, unless you are listening out for it. Increasingly, though, I do listen out, especially on Wednesdays. It's okay, I don't actually sit around the place getting all symbolic about the damned clock. I don't imagine it gradually counting down the seconds of my life. I'm not one for melodrama. It is my expectation that, even at 51, I'm barely halfway through my time. I am slim and healthy. I have never smoked and I drink only occasionally, never to excess. Another 40 or 50 years seems like an awfully long while but I believe I have plenty of time ahead of me.

Sometimes I consider that a little recklessness might have made my life more rewarding. Yet had I not been such a mild-mannered fellow, I would surely have hurled that clock against this laminate wooden flooring long before now and trampled all over the smithereens. These days, I can, at least, imagine such irritation – even rage – yet I am still not capable of feeling either emotion. Not yet.

I sense, though, with a slow evenness which is typical of me, that things are beginning to change.

The young woman next door is braving the elements to smoke. With her right hand, she is holding a hardback book over her head, with her left hand she is dragging busily on her cigarette. She is a nurse, working night shifts. I had little interest in discovering her occupation and certainly did not venture to ask her. But she went out of her way to inform me, when I moved here two years ago and she asked, politely, if I could be mindful of the fact that she might be trying to sleep during the day. She needn't have worried. I listen to Radio Four, except for when anything fictional comes on, but never at any great volume. I dislike fiction, I have never understood the point of it. My wife used to call it escapism. Until she escaped.

As for the girl next door, well, had I not been so mild-mannered, I might have asked her, politely, to be mindful of the fact that I may be trying to sleep during the night, while she is often indulging in so much seemingly strenuous sex. Yet the idea of broaching this subject with her – even now, as things change within me – is an impossibility. During my own sexually-active days, I never quite understood the need to make much of a noise about it. Which is, perhaps, one of the reasons why those days are now gone.

When my wife told me she wanted us to separate, it was quite a shock, I can tell you. Not that it should have been, with the benefit of hindsight. Women often seem to talk about wanting a reliable and steady man but this seems to me to be, almost invariably, untrue.

"Have you been having an affair, Miriam?" I asked her.

"How can you ask me that question, so calmly? So matter-of-fact?"

"Would it be any better had I raised my voice?"

"You've never raised your voice at me. Not in 28 years. But now might seem like as good a time as any to start."

The living room was well-decorated, the house almost fully paid for. I had paid for this living-room, her living-room, and it was becoming apparent that I would no longer benefit from its comforts.

"Answer the question, darling. Do me that courtesy, at least."

"Courtesy!"

Then, I must admit, she swore several times. It was a watershed moment, after which she started swearing, as they do on the television.

"Only you could use a fucking word like courtesy at a time like this!"

"So why do you think we should separate? The mortgage is nearly paid off. We were planning to take nicer holidays after that, now the kids are at university."

"That's precisely why I want us to separate. I can't bear the thought of taking holidays alone with you. Or of being alone with you at all."

"Oh. Oh, I see."

I closed my eyes and winced and pressed at my eyelids. Was this what they called a 'coping mechanism'? You hear a lot of emotional jargon, these days, even on Radio Four.

"I need to feel like a woman again."

"I don't understand what you mean, darling."

"Of course you don't. You never could."

I could never solve cryptic crosswords and I could never fathom Miriam when she talked like this. Not that she'd ever talked quite like this before.

"I had just started making a few phone calls, to my

cousins and such. About our silver wedding party. John and Ruby said they'd come down from Scotland. I'd been looking forward to it very much. Perhaps we could ..."

"Perhaps we could what?"

Miriam was angry now but I hadn't fully grasped quite how angry.

"Perhaps we could see how things go and go ahead with the party, at least?"

"Don't you understand, Brian? I've been fucking another man for the last three years. He's been fucking my brains out on a regular basis and I fucking love it. I don't love him, I don't think I even want to live with him but at least he's got some passion inside him, some energy, some warm blood in his veins."

"Blood heh? Warm blood is it? Has he? Fucking heh? Is that what it's all about, Miriam? Is that what you want?"

I was crying now, for the first time since our daughter had been in hospital and I'd become frustrated that the vending machine wouldn't give me any coffee and that I'd ran out of change for the car park.

"At least you're showing some sort of emotion. Not the emotion I would have hoped for but some sort of emotion at least."

"Which emotion would you have hoped for, by saying these things to me, other than sadness?"

"Anger? Jealousy? Determination?"

Had I not been such a mild-mannered man, perhaps I would have lost my temper. Perhaps I would have wished I had been her illicit lover. Perhaps I would have pinned her to the floor and forced myself on to her. In hindsight, Miriam might have wanted all of this. Isn't this what they referred to as 'passion'?

"Well I happen to feel rather sad about it all, Miriam. Would you rather I feigned some other emotion?"

"Maybe I would."

"I shouldn't imagine it would make a terrific amount of difference."

"I'm leaving now, Brian. I'm going to Stella's for a night or two. After that, we'll maybe talk and make arrangements."

She left the room, climbed the stairs and slammed at doors and drawers as she filled a suitcase.

I met her in the hallway.

"I suppose I ought to phone my cousins. John and Ruby, at least, they had already been talking about booking up a B&B for the weekend of the party."

"Fuck you, Brian," she told me.

"Yes Miriam, fuck me."

* * * * *

Miriam had been wrong to think of me as emotionless. I could be quite a sentimental fool when the mood took me. I'd often listen to our wedding song, our first dance, *Dream A Little Dream Of Me* by Mama Cass. And I even wondered whether Miriam dreamt of me. I imagined that she did. Not out of any great longing or regret. Simply because it was natural to dream of someone you had spent so much time with but who was no longer around. I'd often dreamt of my parents, since they'd died. Chiefly though, I dreamt, as I'd always done, of being lost or late for a work appointment.

I didn't notice any immediate change within me, even after I had moved into this apartment, a couple of months after we separated. I should be rather ashamed to admit it, but it wasn't until they made me redundant that I felt any differently inside my own mind, inside my own skin. The loss of my job altered me far more than the loss of my marriage. There is a certain logic to this, I suppose. One spent more of one's waking hours at work than with one's wife. Yet in this day and age of emotional incontinence, it would seem like heresy to publicly admit that the loss of my job was more significant than the end of my marriage.

I am not a religious man, even though I have a genuine affection for the Church of England and have often thought I would have made a passable vicar. So I have never believed in all that stuff about the meek inheriting the Earth. But even when Miriam left me, I failed to consider my mild manner to be a curse. It was only when the MD of my company told me that I was being made redundant, rather than my more short-tempered opposite number in the department with which we were being merged, that it occurred to me that I may have been chosen for the sack because I could be counted upon to make rather less of a fuss about the matter.

During the six months between our separation and my redundancy, I hadn't told anybody at work that Miriam and I had split up. I failed to see why it was anybody else's business and Miriam seemed content to forward on any relevant post. Yet when Jeremy, the MD, informed me that he was 'having to let me go', I spilled the beans, rather impulsively, by my standards at least.

"It's funny, Jeremy, or should I say ironic? Miriam 'let me go' just as we were planning our silver wedding last year. Now here I am, coming up to my 25 years' service award with the company, and you're letting me go too. It seems as though my shelf-life, as an employee and as a husband, is a little less than a quarter of a century."

I said this in a wry, rather than angry, tone. But I said it nonetheless.

"Oh dear, Brian, I had no idea that you and Miriam had split up."

"How were you to know? You know me, Jeremy, I don't like to make a song-and-dance about things."

"But, last year? Have you told nobody at the company in all that time?"

"No I can't say that I'm one who cares for other people's gossip and I've never considered they'd be much interested in mine."

"Are you okay, I mean are you coping, with the marriage separation?"

"I'm not too sure, to be honest. I've been muddling along with things. I should imagine I'll have more time on my hands to find out how I'm coping now."

"Brian, you will soon find another job. I will, obviously, provide you with an excellent reference."

"Well that is more than Miriam has done," I smiled.

"At least you're able to retain that rather dry sense of humour of yours, Brian. We shall miss that and we shall miss your diligence too."

"Thank you, Jeremy, I appreciate that."

There was an uneasy silence. I detected the ticking of Jeremy's desk clock.

"We go back a long while, you and I. If I'm not much mistaken we started here the same year, in '87?"

"That's correct. Yes, Miriam and I were married in November of '86 and I started here the following spring."

"We must have a round of golf soon, Brian."

"Oh I haven't played golf in a long while."

"Really?"

"No, in fact, I've never played golf."

"That's a pity."

"Perhaps I'll have the time now, to take it up."

"Well one must always look on the bright side."

"One must, Jeremy."

We shook hands and I cleared my desk with the minimum of fuss.

For a while, being out of work felt liberating. Just as it had initially felt to sleep alone. Then the days began to stretch out, especially the Wednesdays. The Wednesdays were when you were glad of the noise of the hailstones. Things began to change though, slowly, evenly. The small things, at first.

When I drank tea, I would often leave the tea-bag in the mug, because I wanted it to taste stronger. Miriam and I had always shared pots of tea – but a tea-bag in a mug was far more satisfying. Less mild, I can tell you.

I bought an Indian cookery book and began to cook stronger and stronger curries. Miriam had always done all of the cooking and though she was quite a dab hand in the kitchen, she'd never enjoyed curries. I considered taking an evening class but this was a daunting thought and, besides, I believed it was more rewarding to be self-taught. It takes a while to gain confidence as a cook. You stick to the recipes at first but it's really rather thrilling when you begin to experiment with different flavours and venture off-piste.

I have thought long and hard about researching my family history, a subject which I am sure I would find fascinating. Yet although I have enough time on my hands, I am reluctant to do so now that my impending divorce from Miriam would appear to leave such a blemish on the family tree. On balance, one probably shouldn't focus on the past in such a way when one is beginning to feel more optimistic about the future.

Still, the biographies I read have become thicker and more challenging. I was no longer content with my reading matter feeling like a gentle round of pro-celebrity golf. As a result, I've begun to have more ideas. I've thought about joining a political party, but am not quite certain which one would best suit me.

Miriam would have been surprised by some of these changes. Not that she would ever know about them. I rarely speak to the children, although they both ring occasionally and have visited once or twice. I don't begrudge them this, they know I've never been much of a talker. Miriam always did most of the talking. My daughter, back from university and living again at her mother's house, seems to have accepted that her mother's new man has more or less moved in. I assume it is the man who fucks her brains out. The brain-fucker, as I refer to him, although only inside my own head, for now. I don't suppose he tends to the lawns as I used to, though, nor the azaleas.

It's those small things that I miss. The lawn, the flowers, our elderly cat, even the monthly weekend drives up to my mother-in-law's. I don't suppose I've seen a country road in more than a year.

But I borrowed a travel book from the library the other day. Norway and the fjords. I've been looking up prices on the internet. Miriam would never have holidayed anywhere cold. As I said, things are changing within me. These Wednesdays won't be seeming quite so long and drawn-out once I'm finished with myself, I can tell you.

5

GUINEA PIGS

She looked like an angel to him. If an angel could ever be seen carrying a small bottle of her own urine. Ethereal beings probably didn't need to pass water. They certainly wouldn't have to sell their heavenly bodies to science. But her pale skin shone, taught against her porcelain bones. Hair up, revealing a long, regal neck. Emerald eyes that hinted of calm. She would have said she looked gaunt without any make-up. If only women knew what men really liked. At least, what he really liked. Something natural, vulnerable.

They were waiting for their afternoon blood tests. He needed to know whether his blood was clean. His ring binders were full of blood disorders, all of which his mind told him he had suffered from at some point or another, usually around 3am, when he woke up with speedway on the telly. God, this whole exercise would be good for him. A clean bill of health. Just to know the Marlboros weren't killing him yet, nor his physical inability to eat five portions of fruit and veg per day. It was a government guideline. He had even seen it advertised on the back of a bus. Did chips count? Mushy peas?

He couldn't keep below 14 units of alcohol a week either but he appreciated the guideline. When were the Government going to tell him how often he could wank? Couldn't the Department of Health appoint a new junior minister for masturbation? He wished they would. He guessed he wanked too much but who could know with such a laissez-faire administration in office? At least that was the good thing about the speedway. If he woke up with a nagging erection at 3am, he never felt like wanking to the roar of motorbike engines and commentators reeling off Scandinavian names.

He wanted to cum on her face. Right there in this spartan waiting room. That would be good for her skin. He had read that in a women's mag on a student's floor in Brighton, once. He had pointed out the article to the girl.

"Semen is full of vitamins and nutrients, it says here. It must be like Laboratoire Garnier inside my balls."

He had soon been asked to leave the student's flat.

The doctor would be buzzing her in soon. To insert the spike into one of her lovely veins. He bet her blood was clean.

It was important to seize the moment. But what to say? 'How's your blood?' 'I like the colour of your urine?' 'Did you know that semen is good for your skin?'

Something away from bodily fluids he guessed. 'My name's Clive and I'm a hypochondriac'. No. She glanced at him, half a smile in her eyes. Now or never.

"Is this your first time as a lab rat?"

A fuller smile. Just the right balance of humour and kindness in his question and in the tone of his voice. He had pulled it off. They were going to get to know one another. Bodily fluids might be discussed; perhaps even exchanged.

"Yes and you?"

"Yeah, well it's an easy way to make a few quid, isn't it?"

"I guess, not too keen on blood tests though."

"You'll be fine."

Gentle but not patronising.

"Thanks. Where you from ... if you don't mind me asking?"

"Dalston."

"No, I meant originally, your family, Thailand? If it's not too forward?"

"Course it's not. I'm an Inuit. Eskimo."

She tried to suppress a laugh at the idea of an Eskimo with a Cockney accent but couldn't stop herself saying:

"Inuit, innit?"

He'd heard this pun, this gag, once or twice before but he laughed now, genuinely.

"I'm so sorry!" she said. "I've never met a ... so Greenland or somewhere?"

"Alaska. A long way from Dalston."

Her eyes were dancing now. She was at ease with him. She believed that being a part of an obscure ethnic minority was a tick in the right box for a man, like having a thick penis or the tendency not to find yoga intrinsically funny.

"Ever killed a whale?"

He laughed.

"No, but I saw the family bring a few in. I've lived in north London, mainly, since I was seven. Not much whale meat there. Not even in the Tesco Finest section."

A man who knew his way around a supermarket, another tick in another box.

"So why did you leave Alaska?"

It was a long story and the doctor left the question

unanswered by summoning her.

"Gracie, would you like to come through?"

"Sure. A cup of tea in the cafe later?" she asked him.

"That would be good."

He hadn't imagined pulling in here. Every time he went to a bar, he thought of pulling women but this place was far more conducive, when you actually thought about it. No need to shout over loud music, no aggressive doormen or fellow drinkers secretly hoping you would nudge their drink so they would have half an excuse to fight you. And it was easier to be open with strangers when a woman was holding her piss in a pot too. The formalities were less necessary somehow.

He hadn't pulled her yet, of course, but he had been entranced by her soft voice, her sweet politeness - 'if it's not too forward' - and especially her slender neck. It reminded him of Anne Boleyn's neck, or maybe it was Lady Jane Grey's, in a portrait of an execution. The picture had haunted him. How could the axeman have severed such a beautiful neck? Perfect. He had just met a sweet, strangely attractive woman and was already thinking of her being beheaded. Wouldn't she just realise that he was filth, lowlife, a toerag? The answer, he reckoned, was 'not if she didn't want to believe it'. And only a filthy, lowlife toerag would reckon on that.

* * * * *

Gracie had been dreading the blood test but as the doctor told her to lie on the couch and roll up her sleeve, she felt a sense of faraway calm. Her mind was suddenly, unexpectedly, fixated on the Eskimo. What a curiosity he was. How she would love to have showed him off to friends, had she still possessed any. He seemed kind and gentle and funny too, of course, but had he been a white man from Dalston, she would not have been so fascinated. Alaska. So frozen, so remote, so primal. She hardly felt the spike in her vein.

Suddenly, her mind was in the arrivals hall of an airport terminal. Flight BA405 from Anchorage. Due in at 22.30, delayed until 23.55. She would not mind waiting for him. She would order another cup of tea in one of those Italian coffee places where they made you speak in Italian if you had wanted a coffee. Why did they make you speak in Italian? Soon he would be holding her in his Eskimo arms. Arms that were born to harpoon whales, whip huskies, that sort of stuff.

Was she really this needful of a man? She had not been aware of it during those recent months of blissful solitude. Sure, she sometimes craved companionship, intimacy, hell, a thick penis - but she could not believe she had been so desperate that her mind should have been sent spinning by a two-minute conversation. 'Behave, woman. You warned yourself that any man in this place would more than likely be a filthy, lowlife toerag with no better way of making a living than selling off his bodily fluids'. But no, not the Eskimo. She didn't want to believe that of him.

She felt the needle withdraw from her with a slight throb, she gasped, the brilliant redness of her blood never failing to surprise her. There was a dizziness as she stood up and the doctor held her arm as she swayed.

Then out into the waiting room, where the Eskimo sat.

"Okay?" he asked, gently, but with the air of a man who could wrestle a polar bear. Were polar bears from the North Pole or the South Pole? The opposite to penguins, she knew that much.

"Yeah thanks." She felt herself blush. Silly cow. If he were the sort of man who could really look after you - financially and emotionally and not just in terms of fighting off wild animals - then he would not be in here. This was a place for losers. Losers like her. Or maybe he was just a drop-out like her? A fellow escapee. A soulmate? Too many magazines, Gracie love, too much shrink-wrapped emotion.

"In the cafe, in an hour?" he asked.

"Yeah but can I ask you something?"

"Of course," he answered, believing her curiosity suggested promise.

"Are polar bears from the North Pole or the South?"

"The north," he smiled. She was endearingly dotty. Well, she was clearly dotty and he wanted to believe she would be endearingly so. His cynicism, like a snug duvet, was being pulled away from him and he shivered, feeling naked. Something was shifting in the firmament as they spoke. He had not felt like this for some time. The fucking L word.

"Come on through," the doctor told him.

He saw Gracie head off to the anteroom to hand in her urine sample. There goes my baby, he thought. And her piss is pale gold.

He would never write a love song.

* * * * *

The rules and regulations of this place had made her laugh. They had emphasised the threat of boredom, urged the guinea pigs to bring in reading matter and DVDs but specifically warned against porno movies. VIDEOS OF AN OFFENSIVE NATURE WILL NOT BE PERMITTED IN THE UNIT. FINES WILL BE LEVIED ON VOLUNTEERS BRINGING SUCH MATERIAL INTO THE UNIT.

Fines would also be levied for illegal drug taking, smoking, using a mobile phone, failing to co-operate with staff, inappropriate physical intimacy with fellow volunteers. So she stocked up on chick lit. There she was, a university graduate, reading what she recognized as being the most unspeakable guff. These were the daughters of Mills & Boon. No swarthy down-market Darcys, here – just fumbling, shambling oafs. She loved the realism.

Gracie was two days into a week-long residential trial. They had told her she would be testing out a drug which aimed to ease lung disease. Some of the guinea pigs would be on smaller doses, some on higher doses, some on placebos. There could be side-effects but as yet, she'd experienced none, and was starting to believe she was on a placebo, as others had reported dizziness and loss of appetite. She guessed a placebo would be the safest of the lot but was almost disappointed that she might simply be wasting the week, rather than genuinely helping to test the effects of the drug. The Eskimo, well, he might not be such a waste of time, however.

There was something promising about him but then there had been promising men before. The poet called Will from Stratford. How promising was that? Okay, Stratford, east London not Stratford upon Avon but she had fancied herself as his muse. Yet he never wrote a verse about her and the poems he did write never rhymed. Poems didn't have to rhyme, he argued. Trust her to find a poet who didn't know the most basic fact about poetry. He was largely impotent too, as a result of 'issues' from a previous relationship. She did not hang around to find out what these issues were, she was already craving a practical man. Not a man who lounged around chain-smoking and chin-stroking, a man who could start a barbecue and stimulate an orgasm, each with a minimum of fuss. Back then, she had felt terrified of mediocrity – in a man, in a relationship, in her life as a whole. Perhaps her standards had been unrealistically high. A friend once told her that what she really needed was a solid, reliable, ordinary bloke. Yet what was ordinary? Who was the most ordinary person she'd ever known? Nobody that she'd known well, that was for certain.

So then came the Jewish carpenter. A sure recipe for New Testament miracles, or at the very least, a man with a clean, circumcised penis who could put up shelves. She used to pull out his splinters with a pair of tweezers and enjoyed the way he winced. And she enjoyed the roughness of his hands, the sweat on his shirt, after an honest day's work. But there was also sawdust in his brain and so she told him she was moving to teach in a school in the north, a promotion, a head of department. She almost started believing it herself. It was true, she was leaving her job, there just wasn't a new job to go to in the north, nor anywhere else.

And so she retreated to her upstairs haven, when she had tucked her father up in bed downstairs and wished him sweet dreams. Because his bad dreams would mean turbulent nights for her. Now that his nights were calm, she could read, and drink Pinot Grigio and smoke menthols and watch makeover shows about people who were too fat, too old, too dirty or too skint, until smug American women, who wore scarves indoors, made them slimmer, younger, cleaner or wealthier. And Gracie preferred the people the way they had been in the first place, when they were less like the smug American women who wore scarves indoors.

Then Gracie would watch a movie and then when the only thing left to watch was the 3am speedway, she began to flick through the teletext and one night she happened upon the airport arrivals pages in the travel section and after she had drifted off to sleep, to the sound of roaring engines and commentators reeling off Scandinavian names, she woke up to realise that you could track the progress of inbound flights from anywhere on Earth, ETAs, delays and landings. So she started to imagine loved ones on long-haul journeys, eating shit food with plastic cutlery, fighting over armrests, striving to stave off deep vein thrombosis, drifting in and out of sleep, and fragmented dreams of her. It became curiously addictive, wondering whether the men returning from Bombay, Bangkok, Cape Town or Rio would arrive home to her on time.

It wasn't a sense of loneliness which had led her to the clinic. Loneliness had ceased to exist, in its place a sense of inner calm. No one could touch her in her upstairs world, no one could disappoint her. It was only when the Stannah money started to run out that she realised she would have to go out and earn again.

It would have been harsh to describe the Stannah scam as an act of fraud, even if the Department of Public Prosecutions might have disagreed. It was a neat piece of thinking and nobody would be hurt. Not Gracie, nor her father, nor her brother. It gave her father a full-time carer, it eased her brother's sense of absent guilt and it gave Gracie a place in which to escape, so as to keep her sanity intact – or so she believed, despite all those imaginary airline passengers.

Her brother, in Canada, had offered to buy a stairlift for his father when his arthritis had prevented him from making it upstairs. But Gracie didn't want her father upstairs and she didn't want to teach sexually aggressive 14-year-old boys any more, either. So she gave up her job, pocketed the ten grand, looked after her father until nine each evening, when she laced his final cuppa with a sleeping tablet and tucked him up in the lounge she had converted into a bedroom, converted his bedroom into a tastefully-decorated lounge and then lounged around there until the early hours, her favourite time of the day.

It was remarkable, and such a relief, how quickly friends and former colleagues stopped ringing and texting when you simply never replied to them. Within six months, the phone only ever sounded once a week, at teatime on Sunday, when her brother rang from Canada. By exaggerating her father's deafness and inventing his senility, she soon stopped her brother asking to speak to his dad. She assured her brother that the Stannah was a godsend and that her father was grateful for her son's generosity, that he knew he was thinking of his old man even though he was thousands of miles away with a stressful job and a stressful Canadian wife who never wanted to holiday in England.

Her father was disappointed when his son seemed to stop ringing but it had been a useful new focus for his restless anger and it had strengthened his sense of affection for his daughter. Gracie knew, too, that he had recently spoken to his solicitor about altering his will. He had appreciated her giving up her teaching career to become a full-time carer. Gracie had looked into the idea of receiving a grant to genuinely become a full-time carer but soon realised that her father, save from his arthritis, was too healthy for that.

And it was not that she was greedy or materialistic, she only wanted for a TV licence, a bottle of half-decent white and a packet of Marlboro greens. She simply wished never to work again or to deal with any of her bitter, bitching, back-biting colleagues in staff rooms where the central-heating pipes seemed to flow with coffee, such was the stench. And she had given up hope of finding a man who would not disappoint her, cheat on her, or, most commonly, bore the pants off her. So, for a time, she had dropped out of the human race, like a failed marathon runner, wrapped in tinfoil.

When the Stannah cash began to subside, she spotted an advert asking for healthy smokers – were you really even allowed to suggest there were such people in this day and age? – to take part in drug trials at a residential clinic. Well, it was money and it beat working, so she applied and was accepted.

It was only on the first morning that Gracie began to appreciate that she might have to hold a conversation with somebody other than her father or brother and this prospect troubled her. So she had stolen herself to adopt a distant approach to fellow guinea pigs, to hole herself up and read lousy books and imagine the clinic as an extension of her upstairs world. Until the Eskimo went and ruined things. That filthy, lowlife, toerag Eskimo.

Before her date in the cafeteria, Gracie found herself looking properly into the mirror for the first time in months. She had grown more pale from her indoors existence, more slender from her minimalist diet and was dismayed, on full inspection, to see a woman who looked plain ill.

* * * * *

A hypochondriac is often said to have a fear of illness. Yet Clive would refute this definition. He was intrigued by illness, obsessed by illness, in love with the stuff.

Before meeting Gracie in the cafeteria, he listened to *Creep* by Radiohead on his iPod. This was the one song which had always been closest to his own heart, and yet in this place, it had lost its resonance – 'I'm a creep, I'm a weirdo, what the hell am I doing here, when I don't belong here?' - because for possibly the first time in his life, he felt he absolutely belonged. For here were some of the finest minds in medical science, focused on how his body was feeling, how it was reacting to the drugs they were giving him. In truth, he'd been surprised that, after two days, the tablets seemed to be having very little effect. Although, the more he thought about this, the more numbness, the more tingling, the more dizziness he had begun to experience. Still, he'd seen one man losing his balance and walking into a door frame, which made him feel rather disappointed, rather fraudulent, that his own symptoms seemed so minor. They had been instructed not to discuss symptoms with fellow trialists, wherever possible, as this could, potentially, skew the results of the trials. Many symptoms could be psychosomatic, they told him, but Clive had always been sceptical about that kind of talk.

Still, he loved the clinical smell of this place, the utilitarian look of it all. And when Gracie walked into the cafeteria, he would have disagreed with most observers, who'd have described her as looking 'scrawny' and 'wan'. Clive, with his twisted sense of aesthetics and with the poetic mind of an Inuit, thought this:

"She is beauty. She is the peaks of the Himalayas, she is a Magritte cloudscape, she is Jeff Labes' piano solo on Van Morrison's *Moondance*, she is the Taj Mahal at sunrise – and not the curry house on Dalston High Road either."

But, having been brought up in England since the age of seven, he said this: "Hello love, you look like you could do with a nice cup of tea."

Trying not to take this comment as criticism of her pallid state, Gracie said: "Yes, tea, tea. I'm glad you said tea and not coffee."

She knew she was already babbling, thinking out loud like one not used to holding conversations. He was still trying to work out whether or not her dottiness was endearing.

"Why do you say that?"

"I think whether you prefer tea or coffee is an essential clue to your personality. I was brought up to drink tea and I think tea-drinkers tend to be decent and honest. Drinking coffee seems pretentious or American or both. All the other teachers at the school used to drink coffee. They even had a godforsaken coffee club and made you feel like a social leper if you weren't part of it. More childish than the children, really. And even though this is England, people tend to ask you whether you want a coffee. You know ... 'do you want to come back to mine for a coffee?', er, you know what I mean? That's an example."

"Well two teas it is in then," he smiled.

"Sorry, I didn't mean to launch some diatribe at you. You must think I'm dotty."

"Not at all," he lied.

Clive did not have the heart to tell her that he preferred neither tea nor coffee. When the *Daily Mail* told him that tea could lessen the threat of cancer, he would drink more tea. When it told him that tea could increase the risk of diabetes, he drank more coffee. He could take or leave either drink – but guessed she maybe had a point and that his unwillingness to take sides in this essential personality test was an indication of a character which was wishy-washy at best, deceitful at worst.

"I also think that tea should be taken strong with no sugar. I wouldn't trust a milky sugary person at all," she said, trying to sound tongue-in-cheek but, deep down, meaning every word.

"Two strong teas, no sugar, then."

Their diets were strictly monitored, in accordance with their drug testing programmes, and tea had to be decaffeinated.

"Decaff tea, my dad would turn in his grave – if he were dead," said Gracie, then laughed nervously, realising she had just made light of her father's mortality to a virtual stranger with whom she was hoping to become intimate.

Clive, however, paid no attention to this comment, instead noticing her bony fingers and the blue veins on the back of her hands. She was probably in her late 30s, he guessed, correctly, but her hands looked sixty. And he liked it. Then he wished that he could hang around in hospitals again, like when his Auntie Vi, who wasn't really even his auntie, was ill. He had never been close to Auntie Vi, but once she was hospitalised, he would visit her interminably, the only visitor ever to outstay his welcome at the bedside of a long-term patient. Auntie Vi was perplexed by his presence and irritated by his lack of conversation. The way his eyes scanned the ward, the way he would wander up and down, catching surreptitious glimpses of drips and bed-pans and colostomy bags.

"Are you okay?" asked Gracie, as they sipped their decaffs. They had only just sat down and yet his eyes seemed lost in memories. Maybe he wasn't as interested in her as he had seemed in the blood-test waiting room.

"Yeah, this place just reminds me of when my Auntie Vi was terminally ill and I spent a lot of time visiting her in hospital."

"Oh, I'm sorry."

"No, it's fine, I used to enjoy it, well, I mean ..."

"Yes, I know, when people are terminally ill their conversation can be fascinating."

"Yes that's what I meant," he said, too swiftly and with a sense of relief that seemed to him to be all too apparent.

Yet Gracie merely observed the exoticism in his dark, narrow eyes, his long hair tied back in a ponytail, his pockmarked, deep orange skin, and she wanted to hear about Alaska, about the Eskimo.

She guessed it may have been her lack of recent social interaction that made her blurt out:

"So you don't really lives in igloos, do you?"

"What, in Dalston?" he smiled.

"No I meant ..."

"In Stoke Newington there are a few, I believe. It's retro-trendy there, but not in Dalston."

Gracie smiled, so wide it felt as if her cheeks were going to split. When was the last time someone had made her smile like that?

"You know what I mean – do they, in Alaska?"

"Not since the early 19th century."

"I guessed that was probably the case," she lied, "but I bet you still kiss by rubbing noses don't you?!"

"It used to be a bit of a party trick of mine, when I was younger, when people knew where I originated from, but I stopped it after I went out with this serious cokehead girl at college. All got a bit messy with the noses, what with the blood and the powder and the snot. She had that thing where she had hardly any septum left."

Gracie screwed her face up at him as he made her smile again. She didn't want to seem too ridiculously smitten.

Clive recalled how he had read the warning about fines being levied for 'inappropriate physical intimacy with fellow volunteers'. Fat chance, he had thought. Well, now he would gladly take the fine, for her.

"So how does an Eskimo end up in north London?" she asked. "If it's not too personal a question?"

"Are you always so polite?" he smiled.

"I was brought up to be polite!"

"I was brought up to kill whales, you can always rebel."

"Okay, so how does an Eskimo end up in north London? I demand an answer, I don't care how personal it is."

"Well, my mother died when I was three and my father was drowned when I was seven."

"Oh fuck, sorry. You see? This is exactly why I'm usually polite."

"It's okay – I've been asked the question a thousand times, it's thirty years since any of that happened. Basically, between the time my mum and dad died, I was in a natural history documentary on the BBC about the Inuit, by a guy called Dick George. Dick stayed in touch with us all and when my father died, and I was orphaned, he adopted me. There were aunts and uncles in Alaska but when the rich white man made his offer, they accepted. I can't say I blame them."

"It must have been a hell of a culture shock, though?"

"Yeah, I guess. I ended up in a posh private school in Sussex. For some reason, I never used to like to tell them where I came from. And I got the English accent very quickly, though more Cockney like Dick's. The kids couldn't decide whether to call me a Chinky or a Paki. They mostly settled on Red Injun, Sitting Bull, that kind of stuff. There were little things I remember, like being frightened by the foil tops on milk bottles."

"I used to have these deep moral objections to private education – well, I'm a teacher, was a teacher, not sure whether I'm an ex-teacher or just a lapsed teacher at the moment. I used to hate it when a colleague took a job at a private school, used to have furious arguments. Then I realised that was pointless, but I still used to fume to myself. Then the more disillusioned I got with the state system, the more I understood, even thought about applying myself but ..."

"So why aren't you teaching just now?" asked Clive, "Just too disillusioned?"

Gracie had already weighed up the strength of the lie that would be just white enough to be acceptable, without scuppering any chance of this thing going any further, should she want it to.

"I gave it up to become a full-time carer for my dad," she ventured.

"God, that's selfless," conceded Clive, with a heavy heart, having never enjoyed the company of do-gooders, "And admirable too. I don't think I could ever give up my own life to look after somebody else."

Gracie could feel her cheeks burning and hoped this might mark her down merely as being shy of compliments, rather than a downright liar.

"Well, Dad doesn't really need much looking after."

"Enough to need a full-time carer, though ..."

"Well, yeah, I guess."

Was she now going to have to handicap her dad more severely just to make her story stand up? Take a hammer to his kneecaps at night so he was incapable of driving his mobility scooter? Drug him up to the eyeballs to make him seem as though he were in the advanced stages of dementia?

Yet wasn't she getting a bit ahead of herself here, anyway? The Eskimo was probably just an incorrigible charmer, a hypnotist of ladies. What with his private education, his links to the TV industry and a rugged fearlessness borne out of an infancy spent on the wild frontier.

So she asked him: "How did you end up in here, then?"

Clive had known this question would come and he knew for certain that he shouldn't mention his ring-binders. Nor the box stuffed full with *Daily Mail* health-scare pull-outs. There must be other reasons to be here, rather than just a morbid obsession with all things medical.

Yet he wasn't quite certain what the best answer would be and he'd already taken far too long to answer Gracie's question, when he said: "Well I kind of needed the cash, I guess ..."

"Well, none of us are here for the love of blood and urine tests are we?"

She smiled, he didn't. For Clive, there was nothing for it but to change the subject.

"Listen," he whispered, as if speaking to a fellow prisoner under the prying eyes of a jailer, "what symptoms have you been getting?"

"That's against the rules ... naughty," she flirted.

"I know, I know, but I'm wondering whether I'm imagining things, a kind of dizziness and a tingling feeling."

In truth, barely a couple of hours of his life ever went by without Clive experiencing dizziness, tingling or far more sinister sensations. Aches and pains which were almost invariably taken to be signs of cancer. Cancer was the hypochondriac's illness of choice; striking, as it could, any part of the body and having a tendency to become terminal with so few obvious symptoms.

"Isn't that exactly why we're not supposed to discuss things?" asked Gracie.

"Oh, you're such a goody-goody, always the teacher!"

"I think I might be on a placebo. Either that or there just aren't any side-effects."

Gracie didn't look well to Clive, her lips were dry and cracked, her eyes a little bloodshot, her skin almost too pale. This woman was beautiful to him, even without side-effects. He felt a lazy horniness.

"So are you just going to be vague and evasive? I don't feel as if I'm getting to know you exactly," she said.

"Why would you want to get to know me?"

"Natural curiosity, boredom perhaps."

Gracie's smile was fading now, her frustration growing.

"Do you have a day job? A career or anything?"

"I've had a few careers ..."

Clive knew he should have thought this through.

How to explain the past two decades without making himself sound like a serial drop-out when he'd been nothing but a serial drop-out – university, careers, women, bit-part jobs, even driving lessons. In fact the only thing he'd never dropped out of were NHS drop-in centres, which he dropped into frequently.

"You're determined to be evasive, aren't you?"

"No, no, I guess I've been drifting a little just of late."

For the past 20 years or so.

"Well, I know that feeling."

Gracie had finished her cup of tea and was about to make her excuses. This was clearly no more than a good-looking nothing; everything she'd have expected of a man who ended up in a drug trial clinic. All optimism was slipping away. The chick lit and lightweight DVDs were beckoning in her cell.

Clive saw her shift in her seat and, gently but firmly, he clutched her hand with his.

Gracie smiled, uneasily. It was shit or bust. He'd identified so many moments like this in his life, and almost invariably squandered them.

"Listen, I think, if I'm honest, that I've suffered from having it all too easy in the past and I've never really found what it is I'm looking for, what it is that I'm good at."

He winced at his own honesty as soon as he'd spoken.

"Okay," said Gracie. "That's less evasive, still vague at this point, but less evasive, certainly. What do you mean by having it too easy, exactly?"

"Well, I went to university and when the course didn't work out for me, Dick swung it for me to get a foot in the door at the BBC, in the natural history department. Ultimately, he thought we'd work together, a documentary about our return to Alaska, my Inuit family, the wildlife, the environment – all sounds a bit self-indulgent now but the head of department loved the idea. Anyway, I was sent away with a cameraman to track down a snow leopard or two. Mainly in Mongolia."

"Wow, I love snow leopards, how amazing ..."

"Yeah, it's a remarkable animal, one of the few big cats that doesn't roar, apparently ..."

"Really?"

Gracie seemed rapt now but, like all of Clive's anecdotes, the punchline would be something of a let-down.

"Yeah, but we were out there for six months, and the producer was being patient with us, but no snow leopard. They're elusive, you see ... and the local Mongolian guide, well, he was something of a piss artist. The day it came to a head we were all a bit hungover, I mean there's not an awful lot else to do out there except drink. When the snow leopard showed up, probably 50 yards from us, well, the camera malfunctioned ... and, well, we'd lost the back-up camera ..."

"Oh no!"

"Yeah, we'd lost it in a card game, so, you know, the whole BBC thing went downhill from there."

"And after that?"

"Well, not long after Dick died. He was 65 but fit and active when he dropped dead of a heart attack, no warning. Terrified me, that did, the suddenness of it all. It turned out he was worth a fair few quid and I inherited a quarter of a million or so, which sounds more than it is, really, but it probably wasn't what I needed in hindsight, lacking direction and motivation as I did. So I fell in love with someone, you know, I shouldn't have fallen in love with, as the song goes, but I wasn't entirely honest with her. The whole thing was very volatile I guess. By the time that episode ended, I was 30ish and the money was running out."

Gracie's expression was difficult to read: part-pity, part-scorn; part-wonderment, part-horror. And it wasn't as if there was anything much more uplifting to come.

"And after that?" she asked.

Clive was feeling the dizziness, the tingling, the shooting pains, for real now. He needed her to nurse him. And he'd like her in a realistic, functional, nurse's uniform, not one of those fantasized sex-shop, seaside-postcard get-ups.

"Well, then there was a business venture, in which I invested my last 25 grand – remember the dotcom boom? Well, it was part of that, except for the 'boom' bit. More recently, I tried to get myself on the straight and narrow, a couple of honest, boring office jobs, a brief engagement followed by redundancy ... a bit of work as a film and TV extra, drinker in pub in soap opera, car crash victim in hospital drama, then recently it's been cigarette testing, sperm donation ..."

"So smoking and, and ..."

"Smoking and wanking, yeah. A professional smoker and wanker."

"Oh my God," said Gracie, but smiling warmly. "Well, that wasn't vague or evasive at all."

And fearing Clive was on the verge of tears, she stroked his hand, then clenched it in hers.

"I really appreciate you being so honest ..."

"I honestly do want to make something of myself. It's just that I never really found out what it was I was good at. I tried writing – a few novels, short-stories – but I just never seemed to have enough imagination, it was always too much about myself ..."

"A lot of fiction is semi-autobiographical," said Gracie, in turn believing in the Eskimo and admonishing herself for potential naivety and gullibility.

"Maybe I should dig the unfinished manuscripts out of the shoebox ..."

They were crammed away beneath the ring-binders and the health pull-outs, but he didn't hold out much hope for them.

'Too honest,' Clive thought, 'usually not honest enough, but too honest this time.' There was never a perfect approach to dealing with such unattractive truths.

He detected sympathy and affection in Gracie but could never have imagined her overriding emotion - which was guilt. Guilt that she'd teased these confessions out of him, having lied about her own predicament. Some might say she'd been no more than economical with the truth over the stairlift scam and her father's really rather reasonable state of health. She'd have called these downright lies, however, and now it was her turn to feel unworthy of the person sitting opposite, however sordid and pitiful his own life's summary.

"I'm feeling dizzy now and I'm getting a few pains," he told her, "I think I ought to go and report it to the doc."

"Yes, sure, I guess you'd better."

"It's been nice, though, I've appreciated it. I wouldn't say I feel better, exactly, in fact I'm feeling sick as a dog."

"Well, maybe we could meet up again, tomorrow?"

"Yeah and who knows maybe ..."

"Maybe outside of here too?" she ventured.

"That would be lovely. I mean it."

She imagined them together — eventually, after she'd come clean about it all — in her upstairs bunker, just the two of them, hiding away from the outside world. Who knows, maybe even finding the strength to re-engage with it one day. If that wasn't too far-fetched.

She watched as he left the room and felt a sense of longing.

And when Clive looked back at Gracie, he imagined himself, once more, coming all over her pale, sickly face. That filthy, lowlife Eskimo.

* * * * *

He'd waited some time for the doctor, his symptoms rising and subsiding all the time, but when Clive was granted his audience, the doctor had been brusque, almost blasé — making a few derisory notes, telling him that he had nothing to worry about and that he must continue taking the drug. They'd test his urine and blood again tomorrow but there was nothing untoward. He despaired of the medical profession sometimes. All those years in university and at medical school and yet, half the time, they were still just guessing. They might as well have employed leeches.

There was no doubt in Clive's mind that he was uncommonly ill, that these were not just side-effects of the drug he was trialling but something truly alarming. He could not settle in bed. He sweated and itched insanely. He craved his ring-binders, which would so often calm him at moments like these. Even he wasn't crazy enough to Google his symptoms, not after he had tried it a few times. There were all sorts of cranks online posting all sorts of unsubstantiated scare stories. The ring-binders were official, medically approved, printed black on white, they stood the test of time. Without them, though, he began to panic. When he stood up, everything blurred. He could not feel his fingertips or his toes. When he touched against anything, he didn't know where his own body ended and the furniture began. He called for Gracie but she was nowhere near him, in the female wing. He called for a nurse but, as far as he could remember, the nurse would only tell him to get back into bed, which was impossible. He was the victim of some terrific fever, some fearful reaction. His brain was overheating and his body was giving way. He craved a needle in his vein. He needed to be knocked out. There was no other way out of this.

With intense, almost supernatural, concentration, he made his way to the door of his room. The corridor leading up to the main medical offices must have been 50 yards long and yet it seemed to him to stretch out like the vast Alaskan snowscapes of his youth. After only a few steps, Clive felt his legs buckle and he fell, hands outstretched, towards a bookcase. This toppled and crashed to the floor with a terrific din and he lay amid the airport paperbacks, the ghostwritten autobiographies and the Jeremy Clarkson diatribes, until a nurse came scurrying towards him, soon followed by the doctor who had inspected him earlier. Other patients blinked their way out into the corridor, to find out whether or not there had been an earthquake.

"Mr George, what on earth is going on?"

"I fell doctor, I have a fever. I'm having a terrible reaction to the drug – but none of you will listen to me."

"Come to my office and I'll explain."

"I'll need a wheelchair."

"Diane, get this ... this gentleman a wheelchair."

To Clive, this truly was the only way to travel. To be wheelchair-bound, immobile, looked after and cared for. How he envied Gracie's father. He hoped that one day she might care for him in just the same way. The dizziness and fever were already wearing off as he was transported into the main offices, helped along by sympathetic glances from fellow guinea pigs and staff. Him, in his own wheelchair, for the very first time.

The doctor closed his office door behind them. He took Clive's temperature, pulse and blood pressure, then looked into his ears and throat.

"Mr George," he said, with self-contained exasperation, "all of your readings are perfectly normal. You are a healthy man - but this drug trial is clearly not for you."

"No, doctor, it is for me. I've just had a reaction to the drug, that's all. Surely that's part of the process?"

"Mr George, you've been taking a placebo."

"No!"

"Yes."

"Well, maybe I've had a reaction to the placebo ..."

"Mr George, because of the disturbances you have been causing for staff and fellow trialists this evening, it is in everyone's best interests that you leave the unit forthwith. I see from your records that you live only ten miles away in Dalston. We'll pay for a taxi to take you home."

"But that's outrageous. You can't just kick me out. I'm here to help out medical science. I can't be thrown out of here. I've made a mess of too many things before. I need to make a go of this."

"I'm sorry Mr George. You seem to have issues with

psychosomatic symptoms. Hypochondria, if you will, and when you filled in your initial questionnaire you would have been asked to declare any such conditions."

"How many times have you sent away a patient, believing they were a hypochondriac and it turns out they've got cancer?"

"Mr George, this is not open for debate. I'll ask the duty receptionist to telephone for a taxi."

"But what about Gracie?"

"I'm sorry?"

"Gracie. You know the pale, thin girl. We've become friends. But I didn't get her phone number or address."

"I'm sorry but it would be against patient confidentiality for us to give out any such details."

"Just pass on my number to her. Here, I'll write it down, please."

"That wouldn't be appropriate."

"But we were ... we had something ... something special ... we were going to meet up away from here."

"Mr George, this is a medical research centre, not some kind of pick-up joint."

"Typical doctor, aren't you? So fucking holier than thou. You've got your degree and your bulletproof job and your chums to look out for you when you fail to diagnose someone who's got cancer, but when it actually comes to helping out a fellow human being, you don't want to know do you? You make me fucking sick."

"I'm going to call security now, Mr George. And our security team will also be handed your images in case you should be tempted to wait around the surrounds of this facility. I'm sorry that it hasn't worked out for you here."

* * * * *

Gracie couldn't find Clive in the common room nor in the cafe that next morning. When she still hadn't come across him by lunchtime, she began to ask members of staff as to the Eskimo's whereabouts but they had no answers. It was not until late afternoon that a nurse knocked on the door of her room.

"Gracie, I know you were looking for Clive George and, to be totally honest, we're not even supposed to ask those sort of questions on behalf of other patients. But I can tell you that Mr George was asked to leave the unit after a disturbance last night."

"A disturbance? What sort of disturbance?"

"I don't know, I'm afraid, and I really can't ask for any more details."

"Would you mind trying to find a phone number or an address for Mr George? It really would mean an awful lot."

"No, I'm very sorry but it is strictly against patient confidentiality to pass on any personal details."

As the nurse left, Gracie felt, briefly, as though she were drowning. As though some distant dinghy had disappeared over the horizon. There was an initial sense of panic but as she lay down on her bed, this soon subsided. Loneliness was no reason to panic. Perhaps it was not even loneliness but mere aloneness. And she had found comfort in being alone before now. Her own company had suited her; it had fitted her rather snugly, in fact.

And what of this 'disturbance'? Perhaps the Eskimo wasn't even as good a man as the charming, lovable waster she had imagined him. Perhaps he was violent and aggressive. Perhaps his true life story had been far worse than the sad little yarn he had spun for her.

However honest people seemed, however bare they appeared to lay themselves, they might always be covering up something more sinister.

The chances of her meeting the Eskimo again seemed slim, anyway. She considered attempting to track him down via social media, although she imagined he would almost certainly prove as elusive as his snow leopard. And once she had finally assured herself that he really wouldn't be worth the pain, that any feelings she had for him would quickly abate, she began to feel calm again. A 'disturbance', that was all the Eskimo had been.

It seemed such a relief not to idealise, such a comfort to resist the temptation to hope. To look on the bright side was to risk the light damaging your eyes. There truly was safety to be found, alone.

And so Gracie looked forward to returning to her upstairs haven at home, with its cheap white wine and its impeccable interior design. For now, she would flick on the television and be grateful to find internet access, where she could find the Heathrow arrivals page and patiently watch the progress of planes, monitoring the ETAs of imaginary friends.

This was, after all, a place to exist for the next few days. A room, more or less as good as any other. Some space of her own, away from all of that.

6

TURKEY TWIZZLERS
FOR THE SOUL

Of all the Sunday mornings in a long time, this had been the most truly Sunday morningish of all. Which had a lot to do with the fact that Saturday night had been so truly, properly, Saturday nightish. A Saturday night he would have been proud of, even in his late teens or early 20s.

He had not been able to take her out for dinner, of course, but in some respects, this had been an advantage. He had been able to drink alcopops inconspicuously, without social stigma, and they could drink more heavily than they might otherwise have done. They ended up in a bar, somewhere between a pub and a club and, after a few Hooches, he had egged her on to the minimalist dancefloor just at the right moment in the DJ's set. *Rock Lobster* by the B52s, daft but compulsively danceable. They were both drunk enough to dance uninhibitedly, which is the only way to dance, but not so drunk as to collide with people and risk a glassing. Plenty of eye contact, a couple of those John Travolta and Uma Thurman *Pulp Fiction* hand gestures. The ironic and the erotic in perfect harmony. In fact, she had an Uma-type bob, Uma-type attitude. Half an hour of smooth moves to retro tunes – *Suspicious Minds*, *Green Onions*, *Peace Frog* – and the deal was closed, the cab to his place ordered.

The drunken sex had felt good but, significantly, the post-coital intimacy had felt even better and then the hungover 9am sex was eager, hungry, verging on desperate. Blood rising everywhere, thumping in his temples, surging through his groin.

And Sunday morning had drifted, on a lilo, into Sunday afternoon, bobbing gently up and down, until the bedside clock said 13:17. The previous time he'd looked at the clock, at 12:24, he'd simply rolled over, cupped her pleasing little tits, wondered if she might fancy something a little more strenuous than before, thought better of it and slipped back into unconsciousness. This time, though, the calm was obliterated. First of all, he didn't like odd numbers. 13:17 disturbed his equilibrium. A five on the end was okay, halfway to ten, obviously, but not a seven and not a three. It could have been worse – a one or a nine just made him want to scratch his skin until he bled. He didn't need to have a digital clock but, by setting his alarm for 7:01, this ensured he would get out of bed instantly on a workday morning, just to escape such an excruciating sight.

Yet now, early on Sunday afternoon, as he turned away from 13:17, Alice wasn't there. He half expected a note on a bedside table, then he was relieved to spot her clothes still strewn across the floor and hear rattling in the kitchen. The kitchen. Oh fuck, not the kitchen. Why had he agreed to go back to his place, rather than hers, without having prepared for this? If she kept out of the freezer compartment, he might be safe, mightn't he? Mentally, he scanned the shelves of his fridge and his heart sank as he recalled a half-eaten tin of Alphabetti Spaghetti.

He heard footsteps, a clinking of tea mugs, and he buried his head back under the duvet but, as she grabbed his bicep and shook at it, as if to wake him, there was an unfamiliar terseness in her 'Danny!' and he felt sure that he was going to have to have a 'Talk' without even paracetamol or codeine or caffeine to help him think straight.

Popping his head out of the covers and seeing her sitting, naked, on the side of the bed, he attempted a wild stab at flattery.

"Oh, you look … gooood," dry-throated, croaky, seemingly spontaneous, as if this wasn't a diversionary tactic at all.

But she was a woman, not a fuckwit man, and even at this hungover hour, her sensational breasts should have provided him with a clue about that.

"Danny, the really annoying thing is that I was beginning to like you so much that, even if you did have kids, I'd have been willing to try and make a go of it. It's the lies that I can't handle."

"Lies? Kids?"

"I went in the fridge to get milk for the tea and there was a tin of Alphabetti Spaghetti."

"There wasn't any adult spaghetti in the Spar shop …"

"Don't. Do not. Do not make it any worse. I looked in the freezer, and there's turkey dinosaurs – and potato smiley faces – and Moby Dick golden whales."

She spat out the names of these childish frozen foods as if she was reeling off a list of his illicit lovers.

"But I …"

"I looked around for some kiddie photos but you've obviously hidden them, reckoning 'third date, I'll shag her tonight', but you forgot to bin the kiddie food. Listen, do us all a favour, in future, just tell us the truth. A lot of women would be quite happy to work round the complications of a divorced bloke, take on

89

stepkids even, you'd be surprised. Okay, so I said it was a pleasant shock, at my age, to find a good-looking, childless, single guy and I said I'd rather end up a spinster than get together with a complicated man with a bitter ex or whatever ..."

And all of the time, barely listening to a word she was saying, he was thinking 'do I tell a lie that makes her think I am telling the truth or tell the truth and convince her I'm a shameless, desperate liar?' That was the problem with the truth, here. The truth would normally be the last thing on his mind but he wanted to be with her so much that he wanted to give her the truth. If only there was even the slightest chance that she would believe him. And yet lying, and going along with what she had decided was the truth, might be just as difficult.

"How many kids?"

"Er, one," he said, and he surprised himself by having to squeeze a teardrop back inside its duct. A tear of pure frustration, in fact. A tear of pathetic self-pity as far as she was concerned.

"Don't turn on the waterworks. You've been found out, you've got laid and now you've been caught out – at least be man enough to deal with it."

"But I want to see you again. Alice, I love being with you, more than anyone I can remember ..."

"Oh, spare us, what about your ex-wife?"

"I've never been married."

This, at least, a plausible truth.

When she stood up before him and bent over, to collect her underwear, he felt another impending tear, of longing, of lust, of doom.

"So, a boy or a girl?"

"Eh?"

"Your child," she spat, as she clasped up her bra.

In desperation, an image of his niece materialised in his mind.

"A girl."

"How old?" she asked, pogoing her way into tight blue jeans.

"Seven," he guessed. Amelie couldn't have been younger than six, nor older than eight. "Will you stay and drink your tea and I'll fetch you a picture of her."

The panic had straightened his brainwaves. He remembered a school photo of Amelie that his brother had handed him at a family gathering just a few months earlier.

"Okay," she said. "I'm not a child-hater you know, just because I said it would be easier to meet a childless man."

"Of course, you're not, I don't know why I said it, I'm really sorry."

Before she could lecture him any further, he grabbed at his boxer shorts and headed out into the lounge, correctly guessing that the photo of Amelie was in the drawer of the old pine dresser. The little schoolgirl was beautiful – blond bunches, cheeky smile, destined to be a breaker of hearts. He was so desperate to please Alice that Amelie's attractiveness pleased him. If you are going to lie, he figured, then throw yourself headlong into it.

"Oh Danny, she is gorgeous, what's her name?"

"Amelie."

"Emily?"

"No Amelie. After the lesbian tennis player."

"Well, it's a role model, of sorts. Times like this, I think lesbianism is something to aspire to."

She smiled.

He smiled back.

But then as she looked at Amelie's photo again, the

smile fell from Alice's face and she appeared to be cross, even crosser than she had when she'd discovered the turkey dinosaurs. Turkey dinosaurs which might as well have been the imperishable false teeth from a victim of the Acid Bath Murderer, John George Haigh.

"It's one thing lying to me to get me into bed, it's another thing denying the existence of a little girl as beautiful as this. I'm sorry, Danny, that's just callous."

She slammed her mug of tea down on the bedside table and the thud of china on timber reminded him that he still hadn't taken any paracetamol.

"Goodbye, Danny."

He pulled the duvet back up above his head and there he lay – a liar when he was truthful, callous when he told a white lie. She made a point of crashing the front door shut with malicious force.

He screamed out 'fuck you!' – though not until he was convinced she would be out of earshot because you never knew with women, they could always change their mind and give you a second chance. Especially when the sex had been that good.

* * * * *

On 46 different occasions he'd started writing text messages to Alice. Nineteen times he had actually finished the message and his hand had hovered over the 'send' button for somewhere between five seconds and three-quarters of an hour. Sometimes the text messages had spelled out, or hinted at, the truth. Yet the truth had always been too ridiculous to send as a text message. Sometimes the texts had gone along with his original lie. He almost made himself believe that his niece really was his estranged daughter. But the lie, like most lies, only had such limited shelf-life, as if the text message should end with 'BEST BEFORE: APRIL 23'. Sometimes the text messages had ignored both the lie and the truth, had been jaunty and glib, sincere and regretful or indifferent and horny. Yet each one had been deleted, the modern-day embers of love letters unsent, toasted in the hearth.

All week, he'd worked longer hours, though never without checking all his email accounts at least once every half-hour. He hadn't gone out. He had drank himself into a stupor home alone on Saturday, having cancelled arrangements with friends. Nothing had affected him quite like this in years. Possibly since teenage times. Was it just Alice, her vivacity, her beauty and that warm heart, wrapped in barbed wire for security. Or was it the syndrome, the disorder, the whatever-the-fuck-you-wanted-to-call-it? Maybe he should head straight to the supermarket and try again, for the hundredth time. Maybe seek help. Maybe see how the truth would go down with Alice.

It was already too late to make the next career move at work, since he'd snubbed the offer of the job that would have taken him on to the dinner-party circuit. Pretty soon, it would be too late to find a woman too. He was almost 40. Tick followed tock followed tick followed tock. Although, masochistically, all of his watches and clocks were digital. Those odd numbers often seemed to be the only method of preventing him from grinding to a halt.

Had the oven not packed up, he wouldn't have ventured out on the Sunday evening, either. Even though the walls of his home felt as if they were closing in towards crushing point. Was it significant that the modern decor his sister had chosen for this place, seemed so cold, so clinical, so antiseptic?

Yet when he did leave his home, he opted for the Swan & Cuckoo, four miles away. Alice's local. Well, he told himself, he'd run out of places in his neck of the woods where he had never eaten before. That was the reason he'd chosen the Swan & Cuckoo. He wasn't hoping she'd pop in, even though he knew she was a regular. He wasn't even trying to gain a little Dutch courage so he could knock at her door.

The pub was empty and quiet. He headed straight for the old-school jukebox, which he knew to be excellent. *Every Day Is Like Sunday* by Morrissey first. Music to reflect, not alter, his mood.

The barmaid was a fat, sad Goth. He risked asking for a Smirnoff Ice. Took a bar-stool, a menu and then the plunge.

"Are you serving food?"

"Yeah. What d'ya want?"

Some basic manners, he thought. But he wasn't in a position of strength here.

"Do you know what?" he smiled, attempting spontaneity, "I really fancy some chicken nuggets and chips."

"What? Off the children's menu?"

"Yeah, sorry I know it's weird, just got a craving for them."

"We don't serve kids' food after six."

Often they smiled when he asked but this barmaid was black-eyed, bulky, lonely, sexually frustrated. More panda than human.

"Do you think, as it's quiet, you might be able to bend that rule, just a little?"

"You really want chicken nuggets?"

"Yes please, sorry, I do."

"I'll ask the chef."

The 'chef', he thought, spare me. The bloke who shoves things into a microwave.

He took a seat in the corner, by the door, and started reading his Sunday newspaper. The Smirnoff Ice wasn't going down too well, even though he'd longed for alcohol. In the paper, where a story should have been, there was the information that a mystery celebrity had won an injunction against the publication, regarding the fact that he'd fathered a secret lovechild. There was an image of the silhouette of a man's head. This emptiness, this anonymity, seemed to captivate Danny. Appealed to him. He wanted enough money to be granted a super-injunction against the world.

His mind had spiralled into a void by the time he saw Alice. She must have entered the pub from the door on the far side with a female friend. She had bought herself a pint of cider but the other woman was leaving already. How long had he been hypnotised by the silhouette in the newspaper?

Now Alice was walking towards him. Eyes dissolved to saltwater when you looked at this woman. Like looking directly into the sun. Her expression, though, was cryptic.

"Danny, what are you doing here? Haven't been stalking me, have you?" she asked with a smile. When he hesitated, her smile turned in the direction of genuine paranoia.

"No, no, no, course not," he said, "just came in for some food."

"Can I join you?"

Again a hesitation. Almost fatal, this time.

"It's ok," and she turned away.

"No, no. Please, stay."

He felt completely panic-stricken. There seemed no

time to think any rational thoughts.

"Danny, I've been thinking a lot about you. Kept going to text you, then stopping myself. Feeling so sad about it all, wondering why ..."

"It was good while it lasted, eh?"

"So it's in the past tense, is it?"

This sounded surprisingly optimistic to him. He realised that, as she'd simply popped over to the Swan intending on a drink with a girlfriend, Alice had not bothered to dress up or make up. She hadn't needed to. The idea of women 'making an effort' seemed to him to be horribly over-rated.

"I was trying not to sound too presumptuous," he said.

"Whenever I ... I mean, I don't often ... not for years really ... but whenever I do find a man I really like, he always turns out to be so untrustworthy ..."

As the silence began to hang, tantalisingly, in the air between them, Panda Girl stomped into earshot.

"Chicken nuggets and chips," she announced.

Alice looked puzzled.

"Doesn't exactly look appetising?"

"No, it doesn't. Listen, sit down, please sit down, Alice ... excuse me, can I have some tomato ketchup?"

The Panda grimaced as if she been told there was no bamboo left in the whole of China.

"Ketchup," smiled Alice. "All of a sudden, your meal, it's Gordon, it's gastro-pub, it's gourmet. Rustic. Why's everything got to be 'rustic' with these TV chefs?"

He'd always adored her sense of humour until now. He'd simply 'got' everything she'd said. But these references were lost on him. He never watched cookery programmes on television. He tried to force a smile but this situation was no laughing matter.

"Listen, Alice ..."

"I'm sitting down, so stop telling me to listen, I'm not going to sit here and not listen to you."

Fuck, she could be so contrary. Which was a quality he'd found endearing at first. He liked his women spiky. Until these sort of moments. He tried the trick he always tried, something his mother once said at the dinner table, imagining himself to be the tiniest particle in a vast universe and telling himself that what he was about to do or say didn't really matter one iota in the grand scheme of things.

"I wasn't lying to you ..."

"Oh for fuck's sake Dan, you've had a week to come up with something better than that. You showed me Amelie's photo, remember?"

"No, I wasn't lying to you ... in the first place."

"Eh? You're really scrambling my brain now. So you weren't lying when you said you didn't have a kid – and you WERE lying when you showed me a picture of Amelie?"

"Yes."

This next part was going to be tough. He hadn't even attempted to explain this to a woman for years - and when he'd tried in the past, the outcome had always been disastrous. It was also true that Alice possessed precious little patience but a dynamite temper. She drove her car like a man. Gladness and fool-suffering did not mix here. This would have to be good.

"So why the picture of Amelie? Is she someone you abducted?"

"Listen, Alice. I mean really, stop being caustic, stop being acerbic, and actually listen for a couple of minutes."

This caught Alice unawares. She rocked back on her

barstool – her bob bobbing, her mouth tightening, her neat, modest cleavage tensing – and she resigned herself to actually listening awhile.

"Amelie is my niece. I was hungover and desperate and shouldn't have said it, but what I said in the first place was true. I don't have any kids. I've never been married or anything like that and I've never had any kids."

"So … turkey dinosaurs? Potato smiley faces?"

Alice glanced down towards his chicken nuggets and her eyes rolled as if she were on the brink of cracking some fiendish code.

"The food in the freezer is for me."

"You like eating children's food?"

"It's not a case of liking it, as such. Um … you know when they say that so-and-so 'has the mental age of a seven-year-old' or something?"

Alice nodded uneasily.

"Well, I have the taste buds of a five-year-old."

At this, Alice spat and spluttered her drink over his chicken nuggets and chips.

"Urgh," he squealed, knowing this minor drizzling of cider was going to make his meal completely unpalatable.

He felt weak with hunger, dizzy with misery.

"You're serious, aren't you?" she asked.

He nodded.

"I mean, you wouldn't LIE about this would you? This would be too weird for a lie? Oh God, I've just thought, the alcopops. I see. I thought that you drinking alcopops was just effeminate."

"No, they're childish too. To be honest, I don't like the taste of those much, either, only the effect. Anything else, any other booze, just makes me sick."

"But, oh my God, I mean you've tried? You know,

you've tried other food? Recently?"

"Chinese, Indian, spaghetti bolognese, chilli, shellfish, white fish, any fish, any steak that isn't cremated, soup, salad, I mean any kind of salad, any sauce other than ketchup, mushrooms, mayonnaise, dressing, Alice, I've tried it all. I just can't swallow it, I gag on it. I've tried and tried. Tried to relax myself, to keep calm, to imagine it's something more familiar, but it feels as though my throat is closing up. Often even the thought of it makes me feel faint and panicky. Just looking at a menu and thinking about eating this stuff, this proper food, it can make it seem like someone has sucked the oxygen out of the room." Bomb dropped, he scarcely felt unburdened. Simply resigned, now.

"Oh, Danny, I mean. It's awful, just awful."

"As awful as if I'd lied about having kids?"

"No ... I mean I don't know. Different awful, I suppose. You know, it would make a big difference, I guess ..."

He knew this all too well.

"No candlelit dinners for two," he said, "no dinner parties with friends, no Sunday pub lunches, no breakfast in bed - unless it's Coco Pops and chucky egg with soldiers."

This raised a half-smile, only a half-smile. It was too realistic for a full smile.

"I mean how do you cope? With work and friends and family?"

"Family kind of know about it, to some extent. I still avoid a lot of things. They think I'm too busy for them, glamorous, in a shit way, which they envy. Friends, well, friends stay at arm's length. It's all food, food, food, having a social life, isn't it? Friends' wives all think I'm a bastard or a commitment-phobe, as they call it, the fact I never seem to hold down a girlfriend. Or otherwise they suspect I'm a closet gay. Then I had to turn down a promotion a couple of years ago, when I knew it would involve a lot of business lunches and dinners. And the worst thing is, I never know what to do with my holiday. They must owe me about six months' leave."

He could not read Alice's features but he could almost brain-scan her through her eyes, all those cells changing colour as she tried to compute a thousand brand-new thoughts, simultaneously.

Last chance now, he knew it. Might as well go out all guns blazing. She wasn't the most sentimental of women but he could try it.

Try the Diana card.

"It's like any other eating disorder," he said, "like bulimia, anorexia ... any of those. Just less common."

'Come on, woman, Queen of Hearts, English Rose,' he thought, 'you're female, you must be a sucker for Lady Di.' His lack of long-term relationships may not have been entirely down to his food issues.

Alice was considering this, though, turning the concept over in her mind.

"Not hungry?" she asked.

He wouldn't complain about the presence of second-hand cider on his nuggets and chips. He knew her well enough to know that such a pathetic admission could be the final straw.

"No, like you said, not that appetising is it? Not Heinz ketchup for a start."

Alice shook her head and started texting. She was a compulsive texter. The only irritating habit he'd noticed so far.

"Sorry just got to text Glenda, my neighbour, my mate. That was Glenda, you know, the girl I've told you about, the divorcee, single mum, lovely girl. She came over to the pub with me, so I could talk about you, to be honest. Then, here you were, although you looked in a trance, I wasn't sure if you were just deliberately blanking me. But Glenda said she'd go. Although you are in the pub which you knew was my pub. Which suggested that you're creepy but also interested."

"You've just told her, texted her, have you, this Glenda? About my, erm, disorder?"

He used this word without proper conviction. Alice clearly wasn't going to fall for the Diana card.

"Yeah, sort of, not easy to explain in a text, though. She's my mate, though, of course I told her."

This irritated him intensely. In his own overwhelmingly male world, mates were the last people you ever felt compelled to tell anything important.

While she continued to thumb in words at an astonishing rate, he noticed the panda had been at the jukebox. She'd chosen *Bein' Around* by The Lemonheads. One of my all-time favourite B-sides, he thought.

"This is one of my all-time favourite B-sides," said Alice.

"I was just thinking that myself, honestly, just about to say it, but thought better of it."

"... if you liked me, if you loved me," Alice sang along, seemingly carefree.

"... would you get down on your knees and scrub me?" he joined in. He was a talented mimic. Had Evan Dando off to a 'T', even though it had been several years since he'd last heard this track.

"Well we can certainly enjoy music together," said Alice – and she smiled.

"And alcopops?"

"And other things," she smirked. "It's only your taste buds that didn't grow up."

He risked a smile, too, but her mobile beeped and she frowned. Glenda, it seemed, might be one of those guerilla girlfriend-of-girlfriends, always liable to ambush you.

"What's up?"

"Nothing, just texting Glenda."

"What does she say?"

But Alice was already too busy texting again.

Hadn't he just poured out his heart? Was she going to Facebook his secret or tweet it next? Sometimes it seemed as though an event could not be regarded as having actually occurred unless it had been logged on some form of social media. Like that unheard tree falling in the empty forest. The lost art of keeping a secret.

"Have you decided what you feel about any of this?"

Alice touched the hairs on the back of his hand. She might as well have singed his skin with a branding iron.

"Danny, I never felt so attracted to a man in my entire life as I did to you last Saturday night."

"Fuck. Really?"

"I almost felt intimidated by you. Felt like I'd never be secure with you. That you might be too much for me."

"But that's ridiculous."

"Yes, but who's ridiculous now? I'm not trying to be cruel but now I'm just thinking of you arranging your fishfingers, chips and peas into the shape of a face and writing your name in Alphabetti Spaghetti," she smiled. "So I'm not feeling intimidated by you any more. And the fact that you've felt able to confide in me, about something like this, well that makes me feel like you're serious about me … about us."

"Of course I'm serious, Alice."

"And, maybe, in time, you'll try some sort of therapy? Maybe I could go with you, only if you wanted me to …"

This was promising, more promising than he ever could have wished for. Her phone beeped again and she became distracted, once more. Not a multi-tasker, Alice. It seemed to him something of a myth that most women were.

The jukebox was playing the A-side now, the cover version of *Mrs Robinson*. He preferred it, even, to the original. He'd been in his late teens. The bass-line had just lifted him up and flipped him about like a fairground ride.

Alice wasn't listening to the music, now, though. Danny glanced at his watch, which said '19:59'. He almost pierced a vein in his wrist with his fingernails.

"What's Glenda saying about me?" he asked. "You look perturbed, whatever it is?"

"Yes, well, she's got a question for me to ask you."

Fucking Glenda. He hadn't even met the woman but was already hating her.

"Right, okay, what?"

"Well, it's a pretty crucial question, actually."

"Really?"

"One that will probably provide an acid test as to your suitability for me."

'Stretch me on a rack and thumb-screw me,' he thought, 'Pass me through a mangle. It'd be easier.'

"Okay, okay.'

"One that will reveal your true nature."

"Alice, ask me the fucking question."

"Just a yes or no answer, though, instantly, without any thought …"

"Ask me!"

"Okay, well Glenda said that the next time you go for a Happy Meal, could you save the toy for her son? Because they're doing Toy Story 3 at the moment and it's his favourite."

He bit his lip as Alice traced the outline of his cheekbone with her fingertips, soon wet with his tears. Relief, hope, shame, joy. Fuck, who wouldn't be emotional now?

"It's okay, baby," she said, and she'd never called him 'baby' before.

Alice smeared her forefinger with ketchup and dipped it on to Danny's tongue, just as Evan Dando said that it was a little secret, that it was just the Robinsons' affair.

"There's no need to cry, baby," she said. "There's a child in all of us. No need to cry."

7
DOG MEN

The old man, with the grey skin and the white beard, they call him The Wizard. Although they see him here several nights a week, they don't know his real name and neither do they know that he is mortally ill. Why should they? He still drinks ale and whisky and, resentfully, goes outside beneath the shelter they've built since the smoking ban, to enjoy his pipe – even when it is bitterly cold. It has been bone-chilling this winter and it's late April now. There hasn't even been a spring. They burn wood on the fireplace here and they all wish they could smoke their cigarettes and cigars and pipes inside. They all smoke here. It is a proper drinker's pub. Drinkers and smokers. Alcohol and nicotine, gentle drugs, warming them, killing them softly, with a lullaby.

A bachelor and an educated man, The Wizard is approaching his imminent, unspoken death with philosophy and humour. He has taken to adapting and reciting lines of verse. This night he tells his fellow drinkers:

"If I should die, think only this is of me;

"That all of my nieces shall have new kitchens."

They laugh, respectfully, not all of them understanding the Rupert Brooke reference, but all smiling ruefully at a woman's ability to spend their money on granite work surfaces. There are no women here, tonight. Nor on many evenings. Those women who do drop in are treated graciously, while being left in little doubt that this is not a place for them.

"Old wizards never die," says Bill, "the magic just goes out of their wands."

The Wizard smiles thinly and taps his pipe on the bar, weighing up his desire to smoke it against the chill of the wind.

Bill the Bike is a postman, these days. Bill the Bike nee Bus. The piss-artist formerly known as Bill the Bus. Bill the Bus crashed the No 47 into a low bridge the morning after a night in here and was sacked as a driver. Soon, he became Bill the Bike and he is happier in his new profession, having to speak to far fewer members of the public and having a natural affinity with dogs. The dogs know he's a dog man, they can sense it, so they never attack him and rarely even growl. All the best posties are dog men. Everyone here is a dog man too. The pub has a vast and lugubrious old Labrador, Bernie, much loved by the drinkers but irritable since the smoking ban. He often follows the smokers outside to the shelter to passively inhale. No one ever thought of the pub dogs when they introduced the smoking ban. No one ever offered them patches or counselling. Those who drink here have to leave their dogs at home. Uncommon in her breed, Bernie dislikes too much company, especially the canine variety.

"You're a deep man, Wizard," says Bill, "I used to wish I was deep too. Now I'm glad that I'm not. Present company accepted but deep men never seem as happy as us simple blokes."

"You're not simple, Bill. You have simple pleasures, as do I, but you're very far from simple."

The Wizard is more well-spoken than his fellow regulars but he wears his intellect lightly, never battering his fellow drinkers with his superior knowledge. Never boastful.

"Postmen never achieve anything," says Bill, "and it's mostly emails these days. We'll be history soon. Museum pieces."

"You ought to read Bukowski, he was a postman. Or a mailman, as they call them in the States. I'll leave you … I'll lend you one of his novels."

"Never heard of him, not sure I'd get on with any of your reading matter, Wiz."

"You'd like it. It's not exactly highbrow. It's smutty – but thought-provoking."

"Smutty? Maybe I will borrow it. Although I'd have to hide it from Mrs Bike. When she read that kinky one they're all reading, she had some right strange ideas."

"Oh, my missus has read that one too," says McAnespie, who has just come in from the smoking shelter. "Wanted me to spank her. Wanted to be tied up too. I said I'll tie you up and hide your credit card while I'm at it. My dad used to beat my mum when I was growing up. Now they're asking for it. World's gone mad."

McAnespie, a younger man than the rest, is in the building trade. Was in the building trade. There's no construction now, just a little painting and decorating. He comes here most evenings, straight from work, if there's been any work. Hands the size of woks, grooves in them like an old 45. Worker's hands. He orders another Guinness. There's a sadness about him, since his daughter died, a couple of years ago. He didn't turn up here for a fortnight after it happened. During his absence, Brian the Landlord heard the news, on the grapevine. He told all of his regulars and when McAnespie turned up again, they all lowered their heads towards him and nodded, knowingly. McAnespie knew that they knew and nothing ever needed to be said, suiting all. He was a huge man, with an immense capacity for stout, and would drink a gallon without a trace of it in his voice or in his eyes. So he never felt the need to speak about his daughter here. Mrs McAnespie spoke too much about it at home, so this place was a haven from all of that immutable grief.

This was the sort of atmosphere Brian fostered here. Quiet mutual respect. Sure, there was laughter and certainly the conversation could turn bawdy but if anyone overstepped the mark, Brian simply gave them his look. Everyone knew 'the look'. Everyone understood it. If you received 'the look' twice in one evening, it was time to go home. Yellow card. Red card.

It was possible to penetrate the inner-circle of regulars here, but if your face didn't fit, Brian let you know it.

'You again, is it?' he'd ask, as soon as you walked in. And who'd want to drink in a pub where you were given a welcome like that?

So Brian didn't quite hand-pick his clientele but he might as well have done. This place is pretty much as exclusive as a West End gentleman's club. They are all proper drinkers, they all put a fair few quid over the bar, never nursing a pint. This way, Brian doesn't need too many regulars to keep the wolf from the frost -bitten door, which is the limit of his ambitions. There is no food here, except for pork scratchings and peanuts. Even though the smoking ban has affected his takings, Brian would never go down the food route. He'd never want to alienate his regulars like that. They all stand their rounds in here or otherwise stay on their own. They had been drinkers for many years and they knew the old pub rules.

They may love the darkness of this place, its low oak beams, erected for Elizabethans, who were all practically dwarves by modern standards. They may love its shambling exterior. They may even cherish the cold porcelain and the mildew scent of its dank urinals. But most of all they value the fact that this is an old-school pub by nature. A true drinking man's pub.

Two Jack arrives through the heavy front door. He's a small man, so this is always an effort, especially during these seemingly incessant frosts.

"Two Jack?" asks Brian.

"Thanks, Brian," says Two Jack. And Brian pours two half-pint bottles of ale into a pint pot. The usual.

Two Jack and Bill the Bike are best mates. They first met at The Wheatsheaf 25 years ago but both gravitated here, graduated here.

"Ere, you'll never guess what?" Two Jack asks them all, a broad smile cracking his characterful face, slyness dancing around in his eyes. Two Jack has news and so he holds them all in thrall, a music-hall act about to deliver his punchline.

"What?" asks Bill.

"What?" asks McAnespie.

Even the Wizard raises an eyebrow, quizzically.

"You will never guess!" says Two Jack, shaking his head.

"Tell us then," says Brian. And there's a look, not 'the look', but a look, warning Two Jack not to milk it.

Two Jack takes a deep gulp of ale. A deep gulp which tells them this is going to be significant.

"They've only gone and put a bleedin' mirror in the

gents' toilets at The Wheatsheaf!"

Bill the Bike and McAnespie hoot with laughter. The Wizard taps his pipe repeatedly on the bar by way of applause. Two Jack doesn't quite take a bow but he knows they're glad he's arrived. He knows that nobody is likely to top that line all night and it's not eight o'clock yet.

As the laughter subsides they all turn to Brian. There is a hint of a smile on his lips, yet disgust in his eyes.

"Who'd want to drink in a pub with men who want to look at themselves?" he asks, shaking his head.

"There'll have a website next," says McAnespie.

"There'll be gays," says Dave. Dave who says even less than Brian. Dave who can out-drink McAnespie. Dave who arrives here drunk but never gets any drunker, however much he drinks.

They know enough about the outside world to know you oughtn't say that sort of thing, even if you were thinking it. So Dave's comment is ignored, save for the odd nod of the head. They always knew this place was superior to The Wheatsheaf, now their belief has been confirmed beyond all reasonable doubt. No man will ever look at a reflection of himself in this pub. Not until Hell freezes over. Although each time the door opens, it feels as though it actually might.

They are all perched on barstools now. Dave farthest from the door, then the Wizard, then Two Jack, then Bill the Bike, then McAnespie, nearest the door, best insulated from the draught. They talk a little sport, a little business, a little politics – although Brian never allows this topic to develop too far. Too easy to lose regulars that way. A man's politics are his own private business and not for the pub.

They did have a telly in here once. For about a fortnight. Until old Charlie, Charlie who died, punched a hole in the screen when he became enraged by the smugness of the smartarses on a comedy panel show. Brian didn't even bar Charlie. He resented the expense and the clearing-up but he recognised that Charlie's fist had represented fair comment. The TV was never replaced. They all recalled the story with fondness at Charlie's wake. It was the first Charlie's wife – Charlie's widow – had heard of it all. What goes on here, stays here, as a rule.

The Wizard listens to Bill and Jack dominating the conversation. He went to university, a half a century ago, when few people did. He read English at Oxford. The others don't know this but The Wizard didn't get his nickname simply because of his beard. They know he is wise. He doesn't speak a lot but when he does speak, they listen.

He waits for the pause in conversation, lips wet with whisky, and he turns to Brian.

"O Captain! My Captain! our fearful trip is done;

"This pub has weather'd every rack, the prize we sought is won."

They laugh, not recognising Whitman, not understanding the Wizard's code. He won't be here long now.

"I reckon you ought to start drinking in The Wheatsheaf, Wiz, saying stuff like that," says Brian and they all erupt. It's the time of night when the laughter comes in waves.

The Wizard smiles. They know little of the life he has led. A quiet life. A life which once promised far more than it ever delivered. There will be nobody in his will but nieces. Favourite nieces and inconsequential nieces will be treated all the same. The wake will be held here. All of those nieces will be here, in this alien place. Those who wouldn't wish to be anywhere else, those merely aware of their uncle's wealth. It won't be long now.

Few men can sit on their barstool one final time and say, with any truth, that they hold no regrets. And there is no point for lies now, nor for holding back truths; not with blood in the Wizard's piss and a heavy, permanent phlegm on his chest.

"Tell me, boys, what are your greatest regrets in life?" asks the Wizard.

Brian has never given The Wizard 'the look' before, never needed to. He doesn't quite give him 'the look' now but he is puzzled. Such a personal, philosophical question would normally result in a straight red card. In fact, Brian has never heard a question quite like this during all of his years here and so, suddenly, without ever dreaming of voicing it, he correctly guesses at the Wizard's imminent fate and understands the significance of his question. And so Brian stretches out a palm and allows the conversation to progress, much to the surprise of the others.

"My biggest regret is not driving that No 47 into the bridge sooner," says Bill the Bike, "I've lost a stone on my bike and I feel ten years younger now."

"If only you looked it," says Jack.

"Come on," says the Wizard, "what's your biggest regret, Jack?"

"I'm not one for regrets," says Jack.

"We all have them," says the Wizard. "Some more than others, but we all have them."

"I ought to have paid more attention to my kids when they were young. Maybe then they'd come and visit me now," says Jack, uncomfortably, downing the contents of his pot and urgently ordering "two more,

Brian – and the same again for the rest of these lads."

"Do they live locally?" asks McAnespie, to fill the silence, not out of any great desire to know about Jack's kids.

"The boy's in America and the girl's up north. It's the grandchildren I'd love to see. Two in the States, I've never even met. I get a photo in a card every Christmas. Mavis has been out to see them, I believe, only after she'd, y'know, left."

Bill knew that Two Jack's wife had left him, as did Brian. The others had never enquired whether he had been widowed or divorced. Mavis's exit had been no regret of Jack's. Rather, like Bill's bus crash, he wished it had happened sooner.

"Mine's obvious, I suppose," offered McAnespie, unprompted. "My little girl, you know, who died."

Silence now. Jack wonders how he could have been so neglectful of his children, when McAnespie had nothing left to neglect.

Brian shifts from foot to foot, behind the bar. He looks at The Wizard. You started this, says the look, so it's your turn to speak now.

"Of course it is Mac," says The Wizard, "I never had kids of my own, only nieces, but I know there could be nothing sadder than that."

"Fourteen she was," says McAnespie. "Always my little girl. That's a comfort, somehow. You never really want them to grow up, daughters. And as far as I was aware, until that day, she never had grown up. It's no consolation really but it's a minor comfort all the same."

McAnespie's daughter had hanged herself in her bedroom. Still a child's bedroom, a little too young for her age. He'd been meaning to decorate it for a year or two but it was the last thing he wanted, since becoming a painter and decorator, to paint and decorate in his own home. So a smiling fairy in a mauve dress was strung up from the ceiling on a coiled wire alongside his daughter. The girl had been hounded on the internet by people they called 'trolls'. Until then McAnespite had known nothing of trolls except the ones he'd read about to his daughter, in bedtime stories, not a decade earlier.

Bernie sniffs and slobbers around the big man's feet, as if in sympathy. She knows he's a dog man, she can smell it on him.

"Brian, dare I ask?" The Wizard dares to ask.

Brian doesn't want to get involved in this but he knows, he knows why The Wizard is asking, even though the others haven't realised, despite this unexpected turn in conversation.

"I'll have to play my joker, Wizard, and say the smoking ban. The smoking ban is my greatest regret."

The others laughed at their landlord's impenetrability and his parsimony. Their captain.

"So what about you, your own regrets?" asks Brian, knowing The Wizard must have wanted to have his say.

"There was a girl, when I was young," he says and his pause becomes more than just a pause.

There is true silence now. They had expected more from The Wizard. He'd started this, after all. They nod, they wait. There was a girl. And? It's so quiet now they can hear every whip-crack of the fire, from across the room.

"But I never asked. Never asked her. Never asked anybody anything, really, til now."

They all look into their glasses, no answers there, as many a wife had told them. They look at their feet. They look down at Bernie, sleeping now, so let him lie.

Brian shivers in the draught. He wonders about ordering in some white wine for the Wizard's nieces.

At the far end of the bar, Dave takes his head from out of his hands.

"I think I'm going to have a look in at The Wheatsheaf," he says.

8

WORRY PEOPLE

Guatemalan Worry People are very small, colourful dolls. A person who cannot sleep due to worrying can express their fears to a doll and place it under their pillow before going to sleep. The doll is said to worry in the person's place, thereby allowing the person to sleep peacefully. The person will wake up without their worries, which have been taken away by the dolls during the night.

Which just goes to prove what utter bollocks middle-class, middle-aged women, who consider themselves 'Bohemian', are prepared to believe when browsing around the craft fayres and bric-a-brac shops of middle England.

Dave couldn't remember the exact moment when he'd started to hate his wife. Eighteen years of marriage is such a vast ocean. Who could honestly locate that one particular plankton of misery?

But it was the moment when Sue picked up a pouch of Guatemalan Worry People, and regarded them with a look of such benign delight. That was the incident which crystallised his mind. That was the specific moment when he knew he had to divorce her.

It had been a long weekend away in the Cotswolds. A weekend of her choosing. A time just for 'us', she'd said. Time to redress the 'work-life balance' a little. Oh how he'd dreaded it. The unspoken knowledge that he would feel compelled to try and have sex with a woman who physically repulsed him. Yet, worse even than that, was the slow torture of having to spend 'quality time' alone with her, in pubs, restaurants and antique emporiums.

He'd long since grown to loathe family holidays with their two teenage children. Yet at least on those occasions the burden was spread, his own misery eclipsed by that of his daughter and son. But as he drove into a car park outside a barn conversion somewhere near Chipping Campden, there was nowhere to hide. 'Convert all barn conversions back into barns', he'd thought, 'that would get the country moving again'.

Instead, though, he had to endure an entire barn-sized premises crammed with cartooned mugs, saccharine slogans etched into faded wood, CDs of panpipe music, bejewelled shot glasses, homemade chutneys, Guatemalan Worry People.

It wasn't as if he hadn't countenanced the idea of leaving her before. He'd frequently weighed up the pros and cons, first during moments of idle fantasy, then during long evenings of intent contemplation, while she watched property shows on cable TV, repeated herself endlessly to friends and family on the telephone and, more recently, sat on her laptop having discovered Facebook.

But although he wouldn't describe himself as being overly materialistic (then again, who would?) the financial implications were always such an overwhelmingly weighty 'con'.

Then there was the prospect of being a part-time dad, which terrified him. It wasn't the idea of seeing less of his kids. He guessed he wouldn't see much less of them than he already did, what with his work and their school. No, it was the notion of being expected to actively come up with ideas of what to 'do' with the kids. And the older they got, the more frightening this prospect became.

Living in a small flat rather than a large-ish house was actually noted down as a 'pro'. There'd be so little property to be handy around. Dave had often wished he was one of those blokes who were genuinely terrible at DIY, like his mate Dave, who was so utterly useless that his wife never even nagged him about it. Instead he'd hated handiwork, despite having a reasonable aptitude for it.

Having free rein of the remote control would be blissful, too, of course. Not the adult channels. Certainly not since his daughter, Ella, had closed in on the same sort of age as those wretched, muted, masturbating phone-sex girls. Dave was working off distant memory, admittedly, but what made those TV women believe that people on the brink of ecstasy would ever have a facial expression like THAT? They always looked as if they had just stubbed a toe.

Dave realised that, some time ago, he had simply stopped thinking about sex altogether. He had not just stopped wanting his wife, he'd stopped even wanting to want her. And he'd stopped wanting any other woman either. When he weighed up all those pros and cons of divorce and separation, making love to some-body else didn't feature in either list. This was what she'd done to him. Just by being in the same house. He used to love women in every imaginable away, yet now he was steaming headlong into misogyny.

Even Ella's raging hormones made him want to hide away. It was his daughter as well as his wife, who made him think seriously about making a retreat in his shed, as other men were supposed to have done. He began to believe this was the compromise he'd been looking for. A separate shed life. There, he could drink as much ale as he liked, without disapproving looks. In the mirror, he now looked about seven months' pregnant with beer. Realistically, this was a situation which could no longer be reversed. It was too late for a termination. So he'd drink some more, feed his cask-like womb. Tell himself he was drinking for two.

He could move a television in there too. Acquire knowledge. Lose himself in documentaries. It was the history shows that he could watch all evening. The World War Two stuff. Hitler porn. Mussolini smut. Hirohito hardcore.

He could even put up a few pictures. That was something he hadn't done since polytechnic. He might even have that Joan Miro print boxed away somewhere. He'd never met a heterosexual man who cared enough about the look of a room to actually argue with a woman about it. Yet, while being dragged around the Cotswolds and other such places, he'd often happened upon some framed photo or print, some idiosyncratic little work of art, some trinket or ornament, which he'd like to have bought and displayed. Yet he'd long since ceased asking Sue what she thought about such things, now that he valued each breath too dearly to waste it.

The idea of a shed life had been fermenting in his mind for some time now. He just knew Sue would hate the notion, though. Hideously, she might even suggest counselling once more. That was the silent threat which prevented him from even mentioning his plan. Why couldn't she just accept some sort of semi-separation? It's what both sets of their own parents had done, in their own fashion. Her father had simply started spending ever more time at the golf club; his at the pub, until they rarely even saw their wives. Now it seemed couples were just expected to suffer one another eternally. Unless the man was prepared to throw away the fruits of a lifetime's labour for a shot at solitude.

This helplessness, this inertia, had gripped him for some time. Right up until she noticed the Guatemalan Worry People. Surreptitiously, he had read the explanation for these gaily-coloured, knitted characters, roughly the size of children's finger puppets. He had never believed the expression 'toe-curling' to have been plausible in a literal sense until then. But his toes bent and his fingers hurt too. He needed to scratch the bones which itched beneath his skin. And when he noticed the look of fey wonderment on his wife's features, heard her purr and giggle almost imperceptibly, this seemed to hotwire his brain, jolting him into life. Yet Dave said nothing, somehow managing to remain virtually expressionless. In fact, had his wife looked closely, she might even have noticed a faint flicker of brightness in his eyes. Hope of the hopeless, Lord, abide alone.

So it was with a sense of relief, rather than rage or sadness, that he realised, beyond all doubt, that he must divorce this woman, for otherwise he would surely murder her. There was no halfway house, no 'shed life' about it. Not after she'd spent seven pounds and ninety-five pence of his hard-earned money on some ethnic hippy toy for the terminally dumb.

* * * * *

At first Sue thought it might have been guilt which had made her suggest this weekend away with Dave.

She'd shocked herself by even asking him, was even more surprised when he agreed to it (admittedly, with little enthusiasm) and she was almost on autopilot when she went ahead and booked the 'boutique' B&B.

Her heart throbbed when she looked at the guest house's website. How she'd love to spend a weekend there with Alan instead.

Then she decided that some time alone with her husband really was exactly what she needed. Three days alone with the poor wretch, to focus entirely on him, to study him, psychoanalyse him, to convince herself she would go through with it, to imagine how he would deal with the radiation.

Hiroshima, was their code for it. The moment when she would drop the bomb on her husband. She had to pilot the Enola Gay first, as she had far more to consider. Her children were still at home and at school. Then, a few days later, Alan would nuke his own wife. Nagasaki. There'd be innocent victims, utter desolation, but it would be the best thing for everyone in the long run. Peace in our time.

These were Alan's metaphors. He was a historian and author, specialising in the war with Japan, and a committed advocate of the atomic bomb. The second time they'd met, he told Sue he'd once appeared on *Newsnight* to argue in its favour, against some bleeding-heart leftie, back in the heyday of CND. He bayoneted that little hippy, he'd told her proudly. She'd blushed and moistened. One night, when Dave had gone to bed early, she'd stayed up to watch a clip of Alan on the *History Channel*. She'd Sky-plussed it a few nights earlier and there he was, Professor Alan Standish. She paused the picture. His handsome, weather-beaten face. His magnificent caption, in such a rugged font. She laughed, imagining that her husband was upstairs masturbating over the cable TV phone-sex whores, while she was climaxing at the image of an ageing history professor.

She'd laughed, with her mate Elaine, that only she could find such passion in the arms of a much OLDER lover. Alan was seventy now, but as fit as a butcher's dog. She doubted whether her own teenage son could have been any more lustful. Alan was twenty years her senior, while Elaine's lover was twenty years her junior. A carpenter who'd put up shelves and assembled some flat-packed furniture because her husband Dave was so hopeless at DIY that she didn't even ask him to attempt the most basic tasks. "My husband's hopeless at erections," she'd told the well-cut chippy. She was such a one, Elaine. Sue considered her a real-life Barbara Windsor character.

For a while, Sue had doubted she'd ever have the nerve to conduct an affair of her own. Yet since she'd met Alan, talk of their affairs had dominated all of Sue and Elaine's coffee mornings and what they loved to call their 'ladies-who-lunch-lunches'. Their husbands may have been physically spent but they earned enough to ensure that neither Sue nor Elaine needed to work any more, not even part-time.

Sue noticed that Elaine still talked fondly of her Dave, however. There was never the slightest suggestion that she might leave him for the carpenter, nor any other man. As a result, she found it difficult to even hint at the prospect of her leaving her own Dave for the professor.

The two Daves were such good mates. Not that they ever saw one other without their wives. Both Sue and Elaine wished they'd take themselves off to the pub together but all the decent pubs were out in the sticks and they were so hot on drink-driving these days. Sue even joked with Elaine that her Dave should set up a little bar in his shed. Chance would be a fine thing. While she watched TV, or phoned sisters or Facebooked Alan; Dave just sat, sullen, on his sofa, inflating his beer gut almost visibly. He looked at least seven months' pregnant to her. Possibly eight.

It was during evenings like those when she began to draw up lists of pros and cons. Considered whether she really should leave him. She knew Alan would leave his own wife. Knew they could afford a nice home of their own together. Dave could keep this place. Money wouldn't be a problem. Alan wasn't short of a bob or two. TV history professors were the new rock n roll stars.

She wondered whether her lovemaking with Alan would be as passionate if their relationship were no longer illicit. Yet she convinced herself that it would be. She'd heard and read about so many new positions and techniques since Dave had stopped making an effort, several years ago. And she could dress up for Alan, without arousing anybody's suspicions. Seamed stockings, which he loved. She still had an exceptional pair of pins on her for a woman approaching fifty. Elaine always said that, not just Alan. But she didn't believe she could do herself justice without Dave noticing that something must be going on. Her husband already noted, sardonically, that she was trying to make herself look Bohemian.

Soon, though, she could accompany Alan to conferences and on lecture tours. He'd even started getting bookings in America. Over there, they loved his wholehearted support for nuclear armament. Alan had taught Sue that history was so much more subjective than she'd ever previously thought.

And while Alan's wife wanted him to retire, to 'go

to seed' as he called it, she'd encourage him to stay on an upward curve. His career was blossoming in its autumn but behind every successful man was a strong woman. With her at his side, Alan could live the dream. His own BBC series. Even now, with WW2 such a growth industry, the war in the East was neglected. He was enlisting the help of British veterans of the Burma campaign. Those who still had all their marbles.

They'd buy a property with real 'character', like the ones on the cable TV shows she loved. They'd holiday in the Dordoigne or on the Amalfi Coast. There'd be no more teenagers to drag along soon.

It was the idea of telling her kids, though, which terrified her.

"Just wait til they've done their GCSEs," she'd told Alan. Ella was due to take hers next year, David the year after. Then she'd tell her Dave she was leaving. She'd almost convinced herself of that.

"But I'm not getting any younger, Sue, not getting any more patient, either," he'd told her. And the more he appeared on the telly, the more she worried somebody else might nab him. Him, a man with his own captions.

She worried almost incessantly, though, about what effect divorce would have on her kids. Dave called them 'the androids' these days. There was barely a flicker of emotion from either of them, just a constant low hum of irritation with the world and, in Ella's case, occasional Molotovs of fury. They treated their bedrooms like cells, leaving them only to collect trays of food at dinner time.

They weren't bad kids. Not tearaways. Not 'little 'Erberts' like Elaine's boys. They barely ever left the house outside of school hours. They had never been drunk, didn't sniff glue or inject heroin. Yet despite no evidence and without even any significant pointers, Sue was convinced that Ella, in particular, would get into drugs sooner or later. She was headed for university, after all, and Alan had told her all the English Literature students were at it.

The root of Sue's anxiety was her younger brother, Davie. He'd taken so much acid at university that his own promising literary career had been wrecked. Instead, he'd had to spend the past two decades writing for hallucinogenic pre-school children's TV shows. Okay, so Davie had won awards in his field but, in his sister's mind, he was part of some immoral and vicious circle. Kids got to university and started reminiscing about pre-school TV shows from their own nursery days. At which point, they YouTubed them, realised how acid-induced they all seemed and thought 'that shit must be good'. Sue had only ever seen drug-takers on films and TV, so she had no idea how they actually spoke. Yet she believed this whole 'acid flashback – pre-school TV – acid flashback' cycle had been running on a loop for three generations now and she did not want Ella to become part of it. She was already gently nudging her daughter away from English Lit. Towards history. Then, perhaps, Alan would seem like a cool stepdad. Of seventy years old? Oh, Sue. Will you ever be free? And, of course, Ella's drug-taking would surely only be accelerated by her parents' divorce ...

As for David, David Junior, well who knew? Violence and crime was her only guess. Like his father, he seemed only to hate the world. If he were looking for a motive to start his own law-breaking spree, then he could blame the absence of his father. Or his mother. However it would all work out after the split. It was all related to broken homes, wasn't it? Crime figures and family breakdown. They'd always voted Conservative, even in '97. She didn't suppose the Conservatives meant to blame the sort of divorcees she would become. She wouldn't be needing state benefits, after all. But these divorce statistics didn't take any account of that, did they?

These thoughts ran parallel. In Dave and in Sue; in Sue and in Dave. On the M25 and M40, then along the A roads into Gloucestershire. Just as they had done for so many days and nights, weeks and years. Never enunciated. The sort of unspoken fears which turn men towards alcohol and other kindly drugs. And which turn women of a certain disposition towards Guatemalan Worry People in the barn conversions of the Cotswolds.

* * * * *

"Oh Dave I'm sorry, I know they're not your cup of tea, but I'm going to have to buy these."

"Mm 'kay."

"I could get some as a present for Elaine, though I don't think she's the worrying type."

No, thought Dave, she certainly hadn't seemed the worrying type since she'd met that young carpenter that her Dave is convinced she's having an affair with. Oh, if only Sue would have an affair. Then she could've taken her fella to the Cotswolds and left him sitting contentedly in front of the *History Channel*. There was a riveting new series on about the war with Japan this weekend but there wasn't even enough room left on the Sky-plus to record it.

"Buy them, Sue, 'sfine."

"Aw ... thanks, Dave. What'll I tell them, I wonder?"

You'll tell them you have been married for 21 years

to a man you now loathe and who loathes you in equal measure, he thought.

"I don't know, Sue, what will you tell your little Latin American knitted characters?"

At this moment, in a barn conversion in Chipping Campden, the mutual loathing in their hearts reached new depths.

And yet Sue said: "Aw, but what have I got to worry about, really?"

And Dave replied: "Nothing, my sweet."

"I'll put them back, then."

"No, buy the Guatemalan Worry People, Sue," said, Dave with complete certainty.

'Anything to lessen the possibility that you'll want a meaningful conversation with me', he thought. 'I'd pay seven pound ninety-five every day of my life to avoid that'.

* * * * *

This was the most significant conversation either Dave or Sue would have until a minute past midnight, dinner having passed off almost silently, like so many dinners before.

Sue attempted to provoke some gossip about fellow diners but Dave wasn't biting. There was no disguising the fact that none of the other couples or parties in this charming little Italian, across the way from their 'boutique' B&B, could be any more ridiculous than they two.

The bustling nature of the place seemed to make them so conspicuous in their silent hatred yet it had at least allowed Sue to indulge in her favourite hobby of people-watching, while knowing full well that every other woman present would have been sneering at, or pitying, her. Yet a quieter, formal restaurant would only have made their silence more stark. With Dave, you were always left wondering whether or not any particular scenario you found yourself in was the worst imaginable, or whether it could possibly have been even more painful still.

On returning to the B&B, Sue could no longer fathom why she'd packed a slinky little silk nightie, although after such a turgid, grinding meal and such a tortuous wait for dessert and the bill, she'd opted instead to wear her utilitarian pyjamas. The sort of nightwear Erich Honecker probably made compulsory at the height of the German Democratic Republic. They had drank a bottle of wine each over dinner, far more than she would ever have considered before she'd met Alan.

Dave always took a long, miserable dump, last thing at night. So Sue always snuck into the bathroom first, removed her make-up, moisturised, flossed and pissed. Twenty-odd years of togetherness made it less and less tolerable, more truly hideous, to hear her husband grunting inwardly as he shat. The process had been far more repugnant, for both of them, since the onset of his piles some five or six years earlier.

And it was to these strains that Sue, having almost forgotten her earlier purchase at the barn conversion, reached for her handbag and pulled out her set of nine Guatemalan Worry People. All knitted in different garishly-coloured wools. Some male, some female. No more than an inch long. But all smiling reassuringly, in the manner of carefree central American peasant folk. The type who'd meet in village squares and perform unspectacular folk dances on high days and holidays. They were charming, thought Sue. She really couldn't wait to show Elaine. Alan probably wouldn't appreciate them. He was not the soppiest of men, not like Dave had been, at times, when they had courted, many centuries ago.

And although she knew it was daft, and although she knew they were really meant for sleepless children, who were afraid of monsters in the wardrobe or crocodiles beneath the bed, Sue couldn't help but whisper her troubles to the tiny woollen dolls.

As Dave grunted and shat, from behind the insubstantial door of the en suite, Sue told her dolls: "I'm so worried, so fearful, but I can't bear him any longer. I need to be with Alan, all of the time. Alan makes me feel like a woman, you know, like you felt on your wedding night, girls, Senoritas, you remember your wedding night, how it felt to be worshipped and cherished and wanted. But what about the children? What would they think? What would the rest of the family think? Friends? Neighbours? And what about Dave? I wouldn't want him to drink himself to death, the kids would never forgive me and I'd never forgive myself. Oh, please take these fears away."

The chain flushed and Sue slipped the worry people beneath her pillow, just as it had instructed her to do on the tiny scroll of paper. You told the worry people your fears and in the morning your worries would be gone.

She didn't believe it, exactly, but her desperation was such that she wanted to believe. And a fragment of her mind couldn't quite discount the notion. Any piece of driftwood in a whitewater river. She imagined herself drowning in a bottomless ocean as she fell into sleep, Dave snoring, dreadfully, beside her.

* * * * *

When Hector Ortega learnt of his own death, during an eruption of the Pacaya volcano just outside

Guatemala City, it would be fair to say that he considered himself far less fortunate than Sue or Dave or Alan or Elaine or her own Dave, either.

Hector had recently celebrated his 75th birthday, a ripe old age by Guatemalan standards, and had still been in rude health. Having grown up as a fruit-picker during the harsh days of the Banana Republic and having survived several military coups, the 'scorched earth' policy, the 'disappearances' of so many friends and acquaintances (everybody seemed to become mere 'acquaintances' during the disappearances) and then the long, bloody years of civil war, well it really seemed terribly unlucky to have been swept away by a natural disaster, just as peace had finally descended on his homeland and a certain degree of happiness upon his family.

After being informed of his demise, Hector Ortega was soon dismayed further by the suggestion that his Catholicism might have been misplaced. He had always been a good, God-fearing man, despite so much temptation during his younger years. Now he could not help but remember the immaculate calves of the needy young widow next-door nor the wanton loook in the eyes of a girl in a whorehouse during his teenage years nor the riotous, drunken dancing and the intense card games fuelled by shots of Quetzalteca at the local cantina. He thought of Maximon, the Guatemalan folk Saint, famed for drinking alcohol and smoking fat cigars. A Saint who'd been debunked by the Catholic Church.

No, when, after his death, he was greeted by a stern-faced, dandruffed clerk in an office, rather than by St Peter at the Pearly Gates, it appeared to Hector as though he might as well have led a life of sin, for all the good it was doing him now. The problem with established religions, with their rigid ideas of Heaven and Hell, was that they were two or three thousand years old. And the afterlife, it turned out, just like the mortal coil, had changed drastically in the meantime. Heaven and Hell were not being entirely written off but, at best, they were many, many lifetimes away. Like those eternal dressing-room mirrors, further than the eye could see or the mind truly comprehend.

There were, at least, several options open to Hector Ortega. The clerk handed him dozens of leaflets – 'Death – What Next?' and the like, then directed him into a waiting room and told him to read them all carefully and ingest the information over a period which would seem, in mortal time, to stretch for several months.

There was the option of wandering the Earth as a ghost, which sounded appealing at first, but on studying the detail, it became clear that this would be a remarkably frustrating, unfulfilling and futile existence. The likelihood was that you would never once be seen nor detected in any way by a single human being, let alone a loved one you'd left behind. Of course, one could always apply to become a poltergeist, which, with its opportunity for menace and mayhem, was clearly a tempting option for a man who had lived his previous life in such a goodly way. Yet numbers were severely restricted and, in these days of health and safety, the sort of mischief a poltergeist could get up to was becoming increasingly restricted. It was little more than drawer-opening and picture-rattling these days. Even crockery smashing was frowned upon by the powers-that-be.

You could opt for reincarnation but this was a complete lottery. There was no chance of being human two lives in a row, for example. And one could more easily end up as a dust mite or an earwig, than a pampered domestic cat or a performing seal.

So Hector Ortega was beginning to explore the more obscure, localised options when he fell upon the idea of becoming a worry person. Or Munecas Quitapenas as they were known in his mother tongue. This surprised him because, although his wife had given worry people to their own children many decades earlier, he'd never encountered anyone who believed they were anything more than toys – a source of juvenile comfort and fun.

Hector tapped on the office door and asked the clerk: "Are you telling me that worry people really do possess a soul?"

"Oh yes of course, Senor Ortega. Well, the genuine worry people have souls and they possess healing powers. There are many fake dolls knitted, possessing no soul and no powers – but there are many tens of thousands of inhabited worry people the world over. This is not an option open to just any lost soul, only the privileged few. Worry people live in groups of eight or nine, so it is a sociable existence and I hear that being made of wool makes you feel so warm that you're always inclined to help your owner. Would you like to apply?"

"I don't know. To be honest ..."

"Oh one can only be honest here, Senor Ortega, this is Purgatory."

"Well, I'd rather be something more destructive this time around. I've just lived a life of poverty and decency and I've ended up finding it pointless."

"Poltergeists, like rock musicians, are not what they used to be. And it will take you several millennia to train to become a demon, for example, the sort that can live inside a human mind. That leads, in all likelihood, to Hell at some point. And although that might not be every bit as terrible as you've heard, there really is no way of knowing, not from this far away. I do have to recommend to you the option of becoming a worry person, Senor Ortega."

"With all due respect to you, you are only a clerk and I was really rather hoping that I might meet my maker – or at least, make an appointment to do so."

The clerk, who had appalling dandruff and sweated like a man far fatter than himself, laughed heartily at this suggestion.

"Well, the being you refer to as God, but who is actually known as Dave in this place, is just incredibly busy. The waiting list stands at around a half a billion years. Even given drop-outs and U-turners, you're realistically looking at tens of millions of years for a personal audience. It is your right, your Dave-given right no less, to make an appointment. But most of Dave's workload is taken up by administrative officers like myself and this place isn't referred to as Purgatory without reason, my amigo."

"So you would have the final say on whether or not I could become a worry person?"

"Having reviewed the details of your mortal life, yes, I'd make that decision. This is Judgment Day. Although there is always a right of appeal."

And so Hector Ortega ticked a box and slipped into a state of unconsciousness, awaking to discover that, yes, the sensation of being woollen was entirely pleasurable. In fact it was pleasurable quite beyond the realms of human imagination. Think of an orgasm, wrapped inside a cuddle, wrapped inside a duvet, wrapped inside an electric blanket, and multiplied by a seemingly infinite number of layers and then your own imagination might begin to come close.

This might not be the reckless rebellion Hector had been craving but it seemed like a decent reward for his struggles in the previous existence. His fellow worry people were contented too. They were looking forward to doing some good. To helping children lose their fear of the dark, to make them worry less about life in general, to give them the courage to go out and better themselves in a Guatemala which may now have been peaceful but which was still a poor, hard, treacherous place to be.

But instead they had ended up being exported to Great Britain, where Guatemalan Worry People were considered perfectly charming, and then they were transported to a barn conversion in the Cotswolds, and, having been fondled and smiled over by several middle-aged women, they were eventually purchased and spoken to by a woman named Sue.

It was this sort of thing which made Dave – Dave Almighty, that is – so furiously angry. Not that he often found out about such specific instances. There were too many layers of middle-management in the way.

Sue's worries seemed so self-indulgent and trivial to the nine inch-high woollen Guatemalans that none of them wished to speak to her, in the dark, once she was soundly asleep, as they were compelled to do, on this mission, indirectly, from God. The idea was that any flickering memory Sue might have of their conversation would seem like a ridiculous dream, and yet the meaning of that conversation should penetrate her consciousness and ease her fears.

This was their compulsion and yet, for the first time since becoming woollen, the worry people felt irritated and they began to bicker among themselves. Is this what they were here for? To indulge the insubstantial fears of the idle rich, because by

Guatemalan standards, Sue's life was luxurious and idle and ultimately vile.

It was Hector Ortega, to his credit, who agreed to step forward, to emerge from beneath Sue's pillow and address her.

After some soul-searching, it was he who realised that he might be able to empathise with this woman. Recalling the needy, young widow next-door, he convinced himself that despite everything, Sue needed his help. He knew full well that all the money in the world could not make her as happy as he.

"Sue," whispered Hector and she opened her eyes, in the hypnotic kind of trance to which a human automatically falls when addressed by a Guatemalan Worry Person.

"My name is Hector Ortega and it is my duty to take away your worries, as you have asked."

In her trance, the idea of being spoken to by an inch-high knitted character was not, in itself, anything to write home about.

"Thank you, let me explain, I am in a terrible quandary, I have been married to Dave for 21 years but ..."

"I know, Sue, and I know about Alan too. I know all of your worries and your fears."

"So what can I do to make them go away? That's what you're supposed to do, isn't it? Make my worries go away?"

Hector Ortega thought of the needy young widow next-door in Guatemala. The way she used to look at him.

"I understand why you crave being with Alan."

"Thank you, thank you for your understanding – but how would Dave cope if I left him? And what about the kids? They might become delinquents, like it says in the newspapers."

"I can only speak the truth and I must tell you that your husband would be delighted and relieved if you separated – and that your kids, who are good kids, would be happier knowing that both of their parents were happier."

"Oh Hector, this is exactly what I wanted to hear. What I needed to hear. My worries and fears really are going to vanish. I'll come clean to Dave tomorrow, I'll tell him about Alan and if he really is relieved and happy, then we can tell the kids ..."

"No, Sue," said the knitted doll, in a voice which boomed ominously, unbefitting of his tiny stature, "you must stay with Dave until death you do part and you must never see Alan again."

"But you just said the whole family would be happier if we divorced?"

"Yes, Sue, but there is happiness in this life – and then there is happiness in the next life."

"Oh, shit, no. It never said in the instructions that you were bloody religious!"

"Listen, you were after some sort of guardian angel and, in reality, we're the closest you are ever going to get."

"I hadn't thought of you quite like that, not as guardian angels, exactly."

"Well, we were advertised as having supernatural powers to ease your fears."

"But you're just a woollen doll!"

Again, Hector Ortega experienced something approaching irritability.

"Just a woollen doll? You mean to say you often encounter woollen dolls who speak words of wisdom to you?"

"No of course not, but ..."

"Listen, Sue, I'm from the afterlife. It's not quite like they tell you in the Bible. Well, not exactly."

"Not exactly but not far off?"

"Well I can't go into that sort of detail. There is a lot of bureaucracy and my own knowledge is only a fraction of the truth anyway."

"Have you been sent from God?" asked Sue.

"No. I haven't even met the being you think of as God. In fact, I can't even utter his true name here on this earth – but I have been sent by one of his administrative assistants. Quite a junior ranking civil servant, to be honest."

"And you're here to tell me that I should be faithful to my husband, to this ignorant, fat, snoring fuckpig?"

"From my own experience, in life and in death, I can only advise you that this would be the best course of action in the long run."

"But you don't understand. You don't understand how good it feels to be with Alan."

"And you, my dear child, do not understand how much better it feels to be made out of wool."

9

THE CRUCIBLE

"I hate the cold but I suppose it's good weather for a funeral. I mean it should be cold and miserable, shouldn't it? Bone-chilling. It's appropriate. I hate it when you go to a funeral and they tell you they don't want it to be sombre. That they don't want you to wear black. That it should just be a celebration of his life or whatever it is they always say these days. At least that wasn't Uncle Alf's way, was it? He was a miserable old sod when he was alive so why would he want you to be happy now he's dead? But he was kind-hearted, deep down. So when we woke up yesterday and I opened the curtains and there was this blanket of snow, I said to your dad, 'Well, I hope it's snowing up north too because it's good weather for a funeral.' Even though I hate the snow, I hate the cold, usually. I was looking out in the back garden yesterday, and there's a good six inches of snow and I saw this squirrel right near the doorstep, bold as brass. They used to hibernate, didn't they? Squirrels used to hibernate in the winter, I swear. But not any more. I guess everyone's busier these days ..."

"Squirrels don't hibernate, Mum."

"They do. At least they did. That's why they store up their nuts and that. Squirrel them away! For the winter. For hibernation. Still at least the nights are drawing out now. Middle of February. The worst of it will be over soon. March can be cold, I know, but the clocks will be going back in five or six weeks, or do they go forward, I can never work that out, my brain won't compute it, like when I had driving lessons, years ago, I was fine until it came to reversing. Reversing round the corner, three-point turns. Maybe I should have stuck at it. Bit of independence, especially now that Dad's not so well. I really do appreciate you driving me up here, Stephen, I didn't fancy the train. The journey's too much for Dad now. And John just couldn't get two days off work. He's leaving at 5.30 in the morning and doing it there and back in a day. I knew you'd both want to pay your respects to your Great Uncle Alfie, anyway. He was always lovely with you both when you were kids. It was a shame, really, that he was a bachelor, but he always loved seeing his nieces and nephews, he was the same when I was a girl. Hey, do you remember that poem he always used to recite to you?"

"Albert and the Lion."

"Albert and the Lion. Terrifying really, a little kid being eaten by a lion at the zoo. But you loved it. So did John. They wouldn't allow them to publish that these days. Health and safety! You wouldn't be allowed to climb trees either. I don't know what it's coming to. Let children be children. No wonder so many boys grow up to be so angry with the world. Boys need an outlet. They need to expend energy. Most parents won't even let them go to the park on their own any more. It's all PlayBox now isn't it? X-rays, VDVs. That's what your two always ask for at Christmas and birthdays. You really must bring them to see us soon, Stephen. I know it's difficult for you, though. I know you don't get to spend much time with them yourself. Everyone's busy. Busy, busy. Except me!"

The clock on the dashboard read 17:20. Night was falling. The A1 stretched out into the distance. Seventy-two miles to Doncaster. Sheep, snow, pylons, Little Chefs. The traffic was getting heavier but they'd probably arrive in North Yorkshire in an hour and a half.

"So, Auntie Jean isn't coming. Not well enough. Shame. She'd have wanted to be there. But her legs are so swollen now, she can't really get out of the house. Daphne is coming, though, despite the chemotherapy. She's on a second course of it now. I don't know what the prognosis is. She won't say. I'm not sure if she even knows herself. Maybe she doesn't want to know. I think I'd want to know. But I can understand those who wouldn't. Oh, I didn't tell you, Lois, next-door-but-one, her daughter's got breast cancer. Thirty-five she is. Thirty-five! No age, is it? And it's aggressive. No age at all, thirty-five. There's so much of it about. It's all you ever seem to hear about. Cancer. Cancer and redundancy. Pat next-door's boy, Nigel, got made redundant last week, too. When are we going to hear some good news? That's what I keep asking! Maybe once the clocks go back – or forward! Which is it Steve, back or forward?"

"Um, we lose an hour when it gets lighter so they must go forward."

"Really, I thought that'd mean they'd go back. I don't know what I'd do without your dad. I'd be two hours out of sync, wouldn't I! Still, lighter evenings. They always make me happier. When we first retired we thought we'd go away for a month every year – most of January, into February – but it wasn't long, was it, until Dad started getting ill? He tells me he's got years left in him. I hope so. I'd never finish the crossword on my own. Nor would he, though. We're a good team. He's better at the Soodookee than me, though."

"Sudoku."

"I was never any good at maths. They're good though, those. You don't do them do you? You should try them. They're quite addictive. You're busy, though, I know. Do you still do the cryptic crosswords? Me and Dad just do the quick one. Not that we do it that quickly! We start it in bed in the morning. Then finish it when we're having our coffee at eleven-ish. Then, these days, it's not that long til Countdown. Is there snooker on soon? I do love the snooker. Not as many characters these days, I know, but it does fascinate me. The break-building. There's such an art to it. But there's so much psychology involved in that game, too. I'm good at reading it. I can tell when one of them is losing confidence. Even the simple pots become difficult. When they're not potting them cleanly, when they're wiping their feet before they go in the pocket, then you know that something's up. And their facial expressions. Your dad says I'm a witch! I can tell, what's going to happen, though. I'm a witchy-pooh!"

"You should have a bet."

"That's what your dad says! He says you can bet while the match is going along now, not just at the start of the match. On that internet. He's really got into that since you showed him how, Stephen. He spends a lot of time up there in the spare room, your old room, on that computer. I don't know what he does for so long! Probably wants a bit of peace from me, more than anything. 'Will you shut up, woman?' he says 'when it's time to meet my maker, I'll ask for time back in lieu for all the hours I've spent listening to you talking gibberish!' He does make me laugh, still, after the best part of 50 years. I would miss him. I will miss him. Unless I go first. I know, I know, before you say anything, I shouldn't talk like this. It must be the funeral. Got me thinking morbidly. Still, Alfie was 89. Just turned 89. Not a bad old innings. I'd be happy with 89, the way I feel some mornings. The winters are worse, though. You'll find that, too, as you get older! The cold really gets in to your bones."

"Something to look forward to, eh?"

"But you've got to look on the bright side haven't you? You never know what's around the corner. You know, you lost your job, and it's the recession or a depression – they reckon a double-dip depression on the news – but you still found something else. It's not the same as the old job, I know, but it keeps a roof over your head, doesn't it? And the children's. I still think you pay her too much money, though. But still, I know, you want to look after your kids, first and foremost and that's good. I wouldn't want you to be one of those absent fathers. Kids need a dad, especially your Daniel. Boys needs a dad. Girls too, Jessica, too. But boys need a father. Oop – roadworks! I knew it!"

The letters on the number-plate of the car in front read 'FFS'.

"Still, only 60 miles to Doncaster. And once you're at Doncaster, it's next to no time. Do you want to stop at a Little Chef? A toasted teacake or something? I know you never like stopping. I like to stretch my legs and have a wee, but I'll hold on. I'm used to it. Dad never liked stopping on car journeys either. If everyone was like our family, Little Chef would be out of business. Actually, I think they are in trouble, aren't they? Financially? Everyone's busier these days. No time to stop. Even the squirrels!"

"They never hibernated."

"So you say. But you'd never see a squirrel in the snow. And we used to have a lot more snow back then. I remember red squirrels when I was a girl. The grey ones have made them extinct, more or less. Immigrants! Immigrants, eh?"

"Don't start on immigrants, Mum."

"Your Uncle Alf didn't like them, did he? You can understand it. He fought in the war and he came back and the country wasn't his own – but yes I know, there's good and bad in everyone. That's what Paul McCartney said. Although he did take a lot of drugs in the Sixties. People forget that! He's like the Queen Mum now, but back in the Sixties! We weren't all like that. People talk about the Swinging Sixties but it was all pretty tame in reality. Free love! Now it's all internet dating. Have you been internet dating lately?"

In his head, he could hear Ian Curtis singing *Digital*: "I feel it closing in, I feel it closing in. Day in. Day out. Day in. Day out. Day in. Day out. Day in. Day out!"

"I thought it was a bit weird when you first mentioned it, but I can understand why people do it now. Especially at your age. Especially second time round. It's not like you can go out socialising like when you were a kid, is it? I mean, everyone else is married, your mates and your brother and that. And you're all so busy these days. Women, too. They all work full-time. I can't imagine how you'd ever meet anybody any other way. There's no stigma any more is there, like there was when it was lonely-hearts columns in newspapers and that. Have you been on there lately, the dating web?"

"Not lately, no."

"Well you should! You need a bit of fun in your life.

Everyone needs a bit of light relief. Something to look forward to. Since we stopped going on holidays, I think I need something more to look forward to. The grandchildren. I do look forward to babysitting John's kids. But they grow up so fast they won't need babysitting soon. The lighter nights I look forward to, then it won't be long until the snooker. End of April, beginning of May. The Crucible. Different to any other venue. A different sort of pressure. I know it sounds mean, but I like to see them wilt under the pressure! We were going to go, your dad and I, one year. He always said he'd take me, once he'd retired. Stay at Alfie's. Not now, though. Still you probably see more on the telly. Lois next-door-but-one went one year. She said it was a lot smaller than you'd imagine, The Crucible. That was back when Steve Davis was still at the top, when she went. It was after he got married, though. He was never quite the same after he got married. I don't think he ever won it again after that. Your priorities change. He obviously didn't practice quite as much, that and Hendry coming along. He was a right old mizzog, though, Hendry. A mizzog fizzog. Typical Scot, your Dad always said. I know, I know, you'll probably tell me that's racialist as well!"

"Racist not racialist."

"Well you know me, I still think 'gay' means happy. It used to be a lovely word 'gay'. Not any more, though. Miriam, across the road, her son's one. One of these gays. Very well-off he is, though, according to Miriam. No kids! That helps, eh? Not that you'd ever wish them away but ... he designs internets. Webs is it? There's a lot of money in that. The amount of time your dad spends on there, someone must be making a lot of money out of it. I don't think we'd buy a paper anymore if it wasn't for the crossword. Ah, there we go, just a contraflow, we're moving again. Won't be long til Doncaster now. At least John won't get too much traffic in the morning – he'll be up here before rush hour, especially the way he drives. He's got to be careful though, points on his licence. They hide in the hedgerows these days! The police used to be on our side, didn't they? Now all the real criminals get off and they're waiting in the hedgerows with their speed-guns. That's what John says and I make him right. He's so busy with his job and Sarah says he's away from home more and more nights too, but he's doing well, it means he's doing well. He always had direction, did John. Not that you didn't, Steve, I don't mean that – but John especially so. He knew where he was going."

"Yes, he did."

"And sometimes now, I've got to be honest, I don't know where you're going, Stephen. It's great that you've got this other job but I know you don't like it as much as the other one and it doesn't pay as well. I wish you would go on that dating web. Have a few nights out. Play the field! Why not? You're only young once. And forty-five isn't old these days. But sometimes, I know you've always kept yourself to yourself more than John does – you're more like your dad and John's a bit more chatty like me, I suppose, but sometimes I do wonder what it is you want from life. What is it you want from life? What do you want, Steve, more than anything?"

It wasn't that he didn't consider this question. He considered what he wanted more than anything else in life and he thought: 'I want to see a woman having sex with a horse'.

For one dreadful second, he thought he might have said this out loud. But he didn't. In fact, he didn't say anything at all.

10

SPIN CYCLE

Stanley was approaching his third birthday when it became apparent to his father that he was speaking Lithuanian as his mother tongue and English as a second language.

This came as a shock, naturally. Nobody could ever feel comfortable, realising that they had been neglecting their only child to quite such an extent. It had always been obvious that Stanley would pick up certain Lithuanian words from Grazyna. He spent the majority of his time with the nanny, after all, and nobody could have blamed his father for that.

When a healthy young woman's heart had simply stopped beating, without warning, what was the healthy young man's heart which loved it to do?

It had been the bawling of Stanley, at six months of age, which had awoken his father and alerted him to the fact that his wife was stone cold and mauve-lipped, having lain dead beside him for at least six hours. There were times, still frequent times, when he couldn't bring himself to forgive her for dying on him like that. That might sound callous; even more callous than the notion of a young English father who allows his only son to grow up speaking Lithuanian despite his living in London. But he hadn't wanted to have children before he'd turned 30. Of course, no parent would ever – could ever – wish their child away but he had conceived Stanley because he wanted to give the woman he loved what she had wanted. Without the woman he'd loved, Stanley was unwanted. Still adored and revered, in his father's own singular way, but ultimately not actually desired.

Hours at work had been lengthening. His American company loved the work-hard-play-hard bullshit. This meant that they wanted to control their employees' social lives as well as their contracted working hours. At this stage in his life, though, this suited Sam. Many acquaintances, even friends, were muttering that 'he's really thrown himself into his work to try and forget'. Sam wasn't sure that he'd been trying to forget his wife's death, exactly. There simply didn't seem to be too much else to do, other than work. Promises to keep him involved in social gatherings, day trips, weekends away with the kids had, much to Sam's relief, gradually fallen by the wayside. These couples had been HER friends, really, even those who'd originally been his own friends. He'd just been happy to sunbathe in the warm glow of her sociability, to lap it up second-hand and barely even need to make an effort to speak to people himself.

He didn't even like to think about her too much. There seemed to him no point in grief. Grieving was little more than prolonged sulking when you came to think about it. He sometimes wondered how she would regard him now, though. Colder, more distant, certainly not the man she'd married nor the man she'd left behind. And he wondered what she'd make of their son, now, aged three and yet intense, obsessive, complex far beyond his years. Not yet enrolled in nursery school. Speaking Lithuanian. In actual fact, Sam dreaded to think what she'd have made of all that.

For a long while now, Sam had barely seen his son, except for weekends. And then, after a month-long secondment at head office in San Diego, he returned to find that Stanley was speaking, primarily, in a foreign language. Although it had to be admitted that, even in Lithuanian, the boy's vocabulary was rather limited for his age.

Grazyna's English was never as fluent as it might have been, even when he'd hired her. Not as fluent as either of the two other candidates for the nanny's position – the fat, ugly one who spoke Estuary English and the slutty Polish lapdancer type, who spoke English better than 95 per cent of English people.

So Sam chose Grazyna entirely on looks – the fact that her looks were unremarkable. At that point, he simply couldn't have coped with a voluptuous sex kitten in the house – yet he still didn't want to spend any time looking at the lumpen white flesh of the Essex girl.

Grazyna, as it happens, means 'beautiful' in Lithuanian and her parents had clearly been a little optimistic on naming her. She had a friendly face, was a little on the chubby side, and although she'd found a Lithuanian plumber to fuck her in recent months, looks-wise, she was strictly neutral. Aged around twenty-one, she would neither excite nor repulse her boss, and seemed to have a basic affection for children. This was all he'd asked for.

Sam had begun to feel a little jealous of Stanley's closeness to Grazyna, even before he realised quite how limited the boy's English was becoming. It was now as if Grazyna was the sole parent and Sam was some kindly uncle who came to visit at weekends. And pretty soon, Sam felt, it would get to the stage where he'd have been better off buying himself a Rosetta

Stone CD in basic Lithuanian and enrolling his son to a foreign-language nursery school.

When the taxi driver had dropped him off after the journey from Heathrow, a Friday morning rush-hour slog around the M25, and he'd staggered up the stairs to his second-floor inner-suburban flat, he'd staved off the jetlag well enough to have removed the Buzz Lightyear doll from his hand baggage, ready to thrust towards his son as soon as he opened the door and they were reunited. Sam was sufficiently self-aware to realise that his treatment of his son might have seemed negligent, even if, deep down, he didn't feel any genuine guilt or remorse.

Yet despite not having thought about his son too frequently during a rewarding month of hard working and heavy drinking in San Diego, he had surprised himself pleasantly by thinking about little other than Stanley during the 12-hour flight home. Though a quiet child, his son was blessed with a dry sense of humour, while still possessing a good line in wonderment. There was no sense of loss or melancholy about Stanley, a fact his father almost resented. The child loved Grazyna as unconditionally as if she'd been his own mother. The real mother who was never, ever mentioned, but would need to be mentioned at some point in the child's development. Which was, perhaps, why his father had been so lax in ensuring that Stanley learned the English language.

Sam swung open the door to the flat, to find its hallway was a rush-hour M25 of Dinky toys, nose-to-tail in an immaculate circle.

"I'm home," he shouted, expecting some sort of run-up and flying hug.

Yet there was no reply, just the low hum of an indecipherable Lithuanian conversation, between

Grazyna and Stanley, from the kitchen-diner.

Dumping his bags, Sam repeated: "I'm home." When there was still no answer, he poked his head around the door into the neighbouring room.

Stanley looked up from an etch-a-sketch and said: "Labas, papa" - as routinely as if Sam had popped out for a pint of milk, rather than returned from a foreign trip which had taken up around three per cent of the little boy's life.

"He says 'hello, daddy'," smiled Grazyna.

"In English, Stanley, speak in English," Sam said, through gritted teeth, forcing a smile.

"Labas, daddy."

"Hello!"

"Oh, hello," said Stanley, as if the word had returned to his mind like a distant memory.

Sam knew he really should have phoned his son more often while he'd been away but the eight-hour time distance made it so difficult and, besides, the language gap would have made the conversation torturous. It would only have made him feel worse about himself.

He knelt down to where his son sat, ruffled the kid's hair and was rewarded with a somewhat reluctant hug.

Stanley was a good-looking boy, with fair hair and brilliant blue eyes. Everybody said he was the image of his father. It was mentioned so often, and spoken with such certainty, that it couldn't have been mere politeness. Sam couldn't see the resemblance. Perhaps the familiarity of one's own reflection always breeds a certain contempt for it. Perhaps he'd simply forgotten what it felt like to be regarded as anything other than a pitied young widower.

The Buzz Lightyear doll was greeted with limited

enthusiasm. Stanley giggled when he pulled its toggle and heard the toy say, "To infinity and beyond" - but it was the bemused laughter of a child who was listening to an unfamiliar language. Even the TV, playing to itself at a low volume, was tuned to a Russian satellite channel.

Sam told his son how large the American Airlines plane had been, demonstrated its take-off and landing, complete with some expertly-angled banking, as it occurred to him that the terror of flying, which he always used to feel, had vanished recently, now that he no longer really cared whether or not he made it safely home. Sam told Stanley that the traffic on the M25 had looked very much like the queue of toy cars in the hallway. And he told him that, although America was a long way away, it was the country where cowboys came from and Sesame Street and Star Wars, too. He told Stanley that some day, when he was old enough, he would take him on the rollercoasters at Disneyland and up the skyscrapers in New York. The child smiled and, his father hoped, tried to believe in the prospect of these future holidays.

The conversation, while on the warm side of cordial, was, nevertheless, extremely one-sided and when Stanley spotted Grazyna heading into her bedroom, the boy trailed her, yelling: "Baltiniai, baltiniai!"

Following his son into Grazyna's room, he found Stanley greedily rummaging through a pile of her clothes, sorting them diligently into light and dark. Grazyna's underwear was mostly red or black, racier than he'd ever noticed before.

It seemed that Dmitri the plumber's influence may have been widening. Stanley grabbed a bundle of coloured clothing and, ignoring his father, raced to the kitchen, to load it into the washing machine.

This functional appliance had already taken on a magical, mesmeric quality for the boy, well before his father had ventured to the west coast of the States. Now, it seemed, Stanley was obsessed. Once the clothes were loaded, the boy added the pouch of technicolor liquid, pushed the requisite button, pulled his tiny wooden stool up in front of the washing machine and sat – hands beneath his chin, elbows on his thighs – watching intently and excitedly chattering: 'aplink, aplink, aplink, aplink ..."

"Round and round and round, English, Stanley, say it in English!" said Grazyna.

"Aplink, aplink, aplink," said the boy, in Lithuanian, his head spinning, clockwise, aping the Zanussi's drum.

"I think he needs to start speaking more English," said the father.

"I'm sorry, you know I keep trying, I not go to my lessons while you in U.S."

"I know, listen, you must be exhausted, why don't you have the rest of the day off? Do you want to go and see Dmitri?"

"Dmitri! Dmitri!" Stanley exalted, finally snapping out of the trance imposed by the spinning of water and soap powder and whorish underwear.

Clearly Dmitri had endeared himself to his son.

"Nervinti!" laughed Stanley, in a thick eastern European accent, "Nervinti!"

"Stanley!" Grazyna chastised.

Unbeknown to his father, the boy was yelling 'fuck off, fuck off!' Dmitri had considered it a wonderful wheeze to have drummed this expression into the three-year-old.

"What's he saying?" asked the boy's father.

"Nothing, don't worry. Yes, well, if you are sure it

is okay, I would love to leave you two before Monday."

"Until Monday. That would be wonderful. Beneficial," Sam said, as if trying to convince himself. He craved sleep, the jetlag was threatening to pull him under, but he was alarmed by the idea that Dmitri the foul-mouthed Baltic plumber might soon become his son's father figure.

Grazyna hugged the child, but Sam was pleased to note that even she was unable to fully draw his attention away from the fascination of the washing machine's irregular patterns of rotation.

"Hey, I'm getting worried for Stanley," Grazyna told Sam, as she headed for the door.

"In what way?"

"You know he loves the washing machine so good, he don't want nothing more. I worry he is autistic."

God help us, he thought, the woman only knows about 50 words of English and one of those is 'autistic'.

Yet the more Sam watched his child, watching the machine, the more he began to share the nanny's concerns. The spin cycle was met with an insane frenzy and an incantation of "aplink! aplink! aplink!" carried off with the zeal of a Hitler Youth toddler; the Zanussi his Fuhrer.

After the washing machine was emptied, Stanley eagerly passed his father the dresses, leggings, knickers, pom-pom bras, suspender belts and split-crotch panties to hang on the clothes horse.

Then he began to shout: "Baltas! Baltas!"

"What? English, Stanley, speak to me in English – you know, in daddy's words."

Stanley racked his little brains, screwed up his face in frustration and could offer only another: "Baltas!"

He ran back into Grazyna's room and returned with

a small pile of white socks, towels and underwear.

"It's not a full load," he told the child, "not enough."

"Enough!" said Stanley, bursting into tears.

"Hey, hey," said Sam, ruffling the boys hair and then, cursing himself for his thoughtlessness, remembering the power of non-verbal communication on a boy of this age.

So he crouched down on the kitchen's wood-effect lino flooring and slapped his right hand on to the surface. Instantly Stanley slapped his own right hand on top of his father's, the man added his left hand and his son completed the pile with his own left. Stanley yelped with excitement as his father lifted his right hand from the bottom of the heap to the top, then followed suit and they continued this cycle, bottom hand to top, several times, until it was time for them both to start slapping one another, randomly and gleefully, on the wrists. Then the man grabbed Stanley by his ankles and held him upside down, the boy shrieking with delight, the father – denied this joy for a month – almost welling up. They wrestled and they giggled and they re-enacted car crashes with Dinky toys and then the man even relented by throwing the insufficient load of white washing into the machine, keeping his son happily rapt for another hour.

The father and son watched cartoons and taught one another words of English and Lithuanian. Despite his tiredness and despite the outside air being thick with a quintessentially English drizzle, Sam led Stanley out to the off-licence for some cans of warm, familiar beer, which he consumed prolifically, feeling himself becoming better and better company the more he drank; more fun; better in tune with the cartoon characters his son adored. Dick Dastardly, Muttley,

Penelope Pitstop and the Anthill Mob, all dubbed with manic Eastern European voices.

Sam remembered the one time in his own childhood when his father had seemed like a fun person to be with, when he'd been uncharacteristically drunk at a holiday campsite, literally dancing his way back to their tent, late at night, with his son whooping upon his shoulders, earning admonishment from dozing fellow campers, neither father nor son caring in the slightest.

He rarely liked to consider the extent of his own drinking or wonder what his wife would have thought of it. It wasn't as if he'd lost the ability to look after his son, or that he often drank spirits or that he frequently craved alcohol before 6pm, even though steady all-day sessions, when they came about, were always among the happiest days of his life. Where he came from, the statement that a man could 'take his ale' was one of society's highest accolades. And Sam was, by nature, remarkably proficient at this. He was never legless or abusive, nonsensical or overly-emotional; simply a happier, more lucid, more agreeable version of his sober self. Anecdotes tripped off his tongue, jokes were plucked effortlessly from the back of his mind, spontaneous witticisms seemed to appear almost supernaturally. The boyhood shyness, the adult apprehensions, the social inferiority complex – all of these seemed to evaporate. Alcohol, it seemed to him, received an awfully bad press these days. And who were these puritans, exactly? Didn't journalists used to be among the worst – or the best – of the drinking classes?

When father and son began to feel tired, no later than 7.30pm, Sam scooped the boy up into his arms and told him he could sleep that night in his daddy's bed. It was only as he lay and listened to his young son's almost imperceptible snoring that he realised this was the first time he'd slept with another human being for two and a half years. There had been a couple of sessions with prostitutes – one a miserable flop, the other a short, sharp meeting of desperation and violence – but as for literally sleeping with someone, well this was the first time since she'd died. Sam spooned his little son as if he had been holding a woman, blew cool air on to his forehead whenever his sleeping became fretful and, despite his jetlag, it was two or three hours before he joined his son in sleep.

His wife had always been adamant that the infant Stanley should never be allowed to sleep in their bed, because of her fear that it would be a nightmarish ordeal to persuade him ever to sleep alone again. It was important, she often told him, that they had time to themselves. She had been willing, eager, to make love with him only a matter of weeks after the birth, much to his grateful surprise. Maybe she knew, somewhere in her subconscious, that their time together would be short. If so, she'd never felt the need to mention any premonition or to dispense any advice on parenting. She must have trusted Sam as a father, far more than he felt he deserved.

* * * * *

Sam woke up too early, disorientated by his body clock and disturbed by Stanley's fidgeting. Rain was beating heavily on his window. The suburbs of London were drowning into grim winter. He knew he would have to take Stanley somewhere. The ear-splitting horror and the physical indignity of the soft-play area was beckoning him. That or the excruciating sadness of some low-key child-friendly tourist attraction.

"Where shall we go today, Stanley?" he asked the boy over a breakfast of bread and jam.

"Skalbykla!" said the boy, with great certainty.

"What?"

"I wanna go Skalbykla," he insisted.

"In English, Stanley?"

"I no know," said the boy, his face etched with frustration, "skalbykla in daddy words."

"Oh Stanley," said Sam ruffling his boy's hair.

"Skalbykla, Daddy – aplink, aplink, aplink ..."

"Round and round and round?"

"Skalbykla – round and round and round."

"I'll send Grazyna a text," he said, "and ask her what Skalbykla might mean."

But an hour later, after father and son had showered and bathed, there was no reply from Grazyna, who had spent Friday night popping pills with Dmitri and was still several lights years away from reality. Sam Googled the word but spelt it wrongly and could not find any translation.

Meanwhile, the boy seemed only interested in the washing machine, so they loaded up the few clothes Sam hadn't had laundered in his San Diego hotel and Stanley took to his stool to enjoy the show. When the cycle was finished, the child hung up his father's clothes on the clothes horse; then neatly and expertly placed Grayzna's lingerie back into her underwear drawer.

There was still no text message from the boy's drug-addled nanny. The language barrier between father and son seemed insurmountable. Stanley didn't want to watch either of the animated features at the cinema and, unusually, seemed unmoved by the prospect of a trip to the violent, ear-splitting world of the soft-play area either. Instead he gestured out of the window, urging, "skalbykla!" "Let's go daddy, I know skalbykla."

"You know how to get to skalbykla?"

"Stanley knows," said Stanley, with some certainty.

"Walking or in the car?"

"Skalbykla, we walk."

So they wrapped up in waterproofs and headed out, the boy in the unfamiliar lead role, and they turned left on to the street, then Stanley paused and hesitated before dragging his father to the right at the T-junction, then they walked another 200 yards, with Stanley now seeming unsure that he was heading in the correct direction. When he took the next turning on the right, in hope rather than expectation, and found another nondescript residential road, the child began to sob and then he beat his fist against his palm in frustration.

"Don't worry, sunshine," said Sam, "We'll find this place."

But the drizzle was turning into sleet and after they had wandered aimlessly around a few more streets, Stanley ignited into a full-blown tantrum, his father frightened by the sheer force of his son's impotent rage and ashamed that he was unable to entertain the boy for just a single weekend.

Yet despite her mind being off kilter, her grasp of English being slim and her boyfriend feeling furiously horny on his ecstasy comedown, Grazyna at least attempted a reply and Sam's phone beeped.

"Skalbykla the washing shop where they wash the cloth," read the text message.

"A launderette?" answered Sam.

"I think that is right word," texted the girl, just as the plumber was tearing at the sides of her knickers and attempting to mount her roughly.

"I know what skalbykla is Stanley!" said his dad, and the boy's tears began to subside, "in England, we say 'launderette'."

"Launderette," repeated the boy, "skalbykla launderette."

And of course Stanley would have wanted to go to a launderette. How could Sam not have realised something so obvious? A place filled with washing machines would be far better than the cinema or soft-play area. To this little boy, a launderette shop is more awe-inspiring than a theme park. Yet Sam was not an observant man. He'd never been observant at the best of times and, these last couple of years, he had travelled through much of his life in something close to a trance. He had no idea where the launderette was. In fact, he was surprised such places even existed any more. Surely they were only in soap operas? Didn't everybody have a washing machine these days? Even old people? Even poor people? Even the poverty-stricken elderly? How much did a washing machine cost? Three hundred quid? He had no idea, he'd never bought a washing machine in his life.

"Sorry, Grayzna, but where is the launderette? I didn't know there was one near us," he texted.

But the Lithuanian girl had dropped her phone by now. Her knees were behind her ears and she was being pummelled at such force and for such a sustained period of time, she didn't hear the text-message alert. In fact, after half an hour of strenuous intercourse with her muscular boyfriend, Grazyna, her head thumping from the effects of the drugs and the sex, fell asleep and didn't look at her phone again for several hours.

So Sam took Stanley home, tried an online search

for launderettes in their postcode and when this proved fruitless, he dug out an old Yellow Pages from the bottom kitchen drawer and rifled his way through a couple of dozen addresses. The best bet, the only one which looked familiar, was in Jubilee Place, not half a mile from his flat and, with triumph, and then wariness, he said: "I know where the launderette is, I've found it, the skalbykla – at least I hope so."

Alternate bursts of sleet and hailstones were descending now, the north London sky was giving up for the day and turning towards darkness even at two o'clock in the afternoon. So Sam strapped Stanley into the child seat in the back of his car and headed for Jubilee Place. Stanley spotted the launderette before his father did, excitedly babbling 'skalbykla' and other random Lithuanian words. Sam was too relieved to bother chiding his son for failing to speak in English. He pulled up the boy's hood and held him close to his chest as he darted through the apocalyptic weather and into the launderette, then shook off the effects of the deluge like a North Sea trawlerman getting a dog out of a bath.

There were a dozen machines in the narrow shop, six on either side, separated by a wooden bench. Only two of the machines were currently loaded. The place was warm and the smell of soap powder was overpowering, filling Sam's nostrils and permeating his brain cells. He couldn't recall the last time he'd even been aware of having a sense of smell. He wasn't even sure if he'd even smelt Stanley's shit when he'd changed the boy's nappy. Perhaps he'd last been conscious of scent when his wife used to buy flowers for the flat. She liked hyacinths, even though they were considered old-fashioned. Sam had never bought flowers since. Not out of any romantic symbolism, simply because it would never have occurred to him to do so.

By opening the launderette door, he'd set off a bell and, from the back of the shop, he could hear the faint tinkling of a woman pissing, a toilet being flushed and a cheerful young voice calling: "Won't be a minute!"

It hadn't occurred to Sam that there might be some embarrassment factor in visiting a launderette without any washing, coming along merely to spectate. But when the pissing woman emerged from the back room, she smiled as if she'd just opened up the gates of Heaven.

These things Sam noticed about the manageress of the launderette: Her skin was pale and unblemished, the sort of skin he wanted to knead like dough. She wore no make-up and her lips were full, her mouth set almost permanently to 'smile'. There weren't many mouths that wouldn't look better for a touch of red lipstick but this was one of them. Behind a checked apron, her pert tits were upholstered invitingly. They would never be pornographic tits but they could make a man ache. Make Sam ache, certainly. And when she spoke it was with the sort of soft, clear voice you'd wish to awaken you from a coma. Which, in effect, she just had.

"Stanley!" she greeted his son. "Are you here to watch the washing, darling?"

"Aplink, aplink!" yelped Stanley, leaping excitedly on to the wooden bench, down the middle of the shop.

"Yes, aplink, aplink!" said the woman, who was a Londoner but had clearly picked up this word of Lithuanian from the boy.

"Are you Stanley's dad? – oh, of course you are Stanley's dad, you look JUST like him!"

Sam's silent paralysis forced another question from the laundry woman.

"Sorry, sir, do you speak English?"

"Yeah, yeah, of course," he said, his local accent surprising her.

"Oh, so ARE you Stanley's dad?"

"Yes, yes, I am."

And Sam grabbed Stanley from behind in a tight hug as if to prove the point.

"Oh I see, your wife's Russian, then, and you're English?"

"No, that's his nanny. She's Lithuanian."

"Oh, right, wow, it's just he speaks such good Russian – or Lithuanian – and he doesn't seem to speak much English."

"No, it's um, it's unusual I know."

"Is his mum English?"

"She was. She was English. She was. But she left us."

"Oh, how awful," gasped the woman. "I'm so sorry, so insensitive of me."

"No, no, it's fine. I guess he's been in here a few times with Grazyna, then?"

"Oh yes – once or twice a week, hey Stanley? You're my favourite customer, hey Stanley? Oh I love him. Even his name, Stanley, what a name for a young man. I'm sorry, I'm gushing now ..."

"No don't be sorry," said Sam. "Do you mind if I sit down, I feel a bit peculiar."

"Of course, would you like a cup of tea? I'd just put the kettle on."

"Well, um, I guess we mustn't stay for too long."

Stanley was sitting between the two occupied washing machines, his head darting to and fro like a tennis spectator.

"You won't be able to leave for quite a while, it'd break his heart. He'll want to watch them all the way through the spin cycle – only two machines on the go today, Stanley, I'm afraid! – sometimes there are six or seven and it's as if he's in a nightclub, hey Stanley?!"

"A cup of tea would be lovely, then, if you're sure it's ok, thank you."

"Course it's ok. It'll do you good if you're going out in this weather."

As she turned away to make the tea, Sam realised that for two years or more, he'd felt a great comfort in having let himself go, physically. Eating and drinking exactly what he liked, allowing his gym membership to elapse and his waistline to burgeon. He didn't suppose the woman ever expected Nick Kamen to walk in to this place and strip to his boxers but he began to feel self-conscious for the first time in his widowhood and wondered where his gym kit might be.

"Aplink, aplink, aplink!" yelled Stanley as the machine to the boy's right burst noisily into overdrive.

"Around, around, around!" said his father, with something approaching stern kindness.

"Aplink, aplink, aplink!" said the boy, in defiant Lithuanian.

"Aplink, aplink, aplink!" sang the woman, a touch of Debbie Harry in her voice as she poured out the boiling water.

"He's such a gorgeous boy," she said, her tits wobbling, gently, modestly, as she carried the two mugs of tea.

"And he's the image of his father, truly – Stanley you look so much like your daddy."

Her skin was so pale that there was no hiding the

blushing, when she realised what she'd just said.

Sam smiled with sincerity, enjoying her unintentional declaration of attraction but not wishing to embarrass her any further. He watched Stanley as his son regarded the washing machine with wonder. As it juddered to a halt, the boy gripped the wooden bench he was seated upon, held his breath, his eyes widening in anticipation. Just a few seconds more and then the spin cycle would begin. The whirr of excitement, the breakneck speed, the finale to this fantastical show. And even on a wet weekend in the north London suburbs, it felt for all the world as though there was so much to look forward to.

11

MUSIC WHEN THE
LIGHTS GO OUT

First of all it was her voice. A voice which spoke of Silk Cuts behind the boarding school bikesheds. High class, smoky, with a hint of quiet mischief. And strikingly beautiful. It made him want to take up smoking again, almost 20 years since he'd last had the pleasure. It certainly made him want to listen to music again. He hadn't bought any new music for years. In fact, he wasn't sure if he even knew how to. Wasn't it all downloads these days? He hadn't a clue. Whether this was even new music or not, he wasn't entirely certain. There was a dash of long-gone Hollywood glamour and a hint of jazz played in a New Orleans basement bar. He wasn't a music buff but he knew this was outrageously good. As he drove to the office in the eternal drizzle of an English winter, this song was transporting him to some unspecified, unvisited corner of America. Stirring feelings in him like no music had done since he was a teenager, listening to something very different and provoking very different feelings, too. Joy Division and loneliness or The Clash and aimless rebellion.

He turned up the volume on the car radio, so as to be certain he caught the name of the song and the artist and there it was – *Shaken* the debut single by Sabine Dean. So she was new and yet she sounded so familiar. Perhaps that was the trick. He held on to her rhythmic name, muttered the words of the chorus, wished his own voice sounded more throaty and toyed with the idea of stopping at the petrol station for a pack of cigarettes. What would his wife make of that, he wondered. She'd made him quit when they were trying for Samantha. He'd obliged with the minimum of fuss and the cravings lessened over the months and years. But now Samantha was gone; in York to study – and who knew what else. Sammi would be smoking cigarettes, certainly. She'd been smoking for a year or more, although never in front of her parents and the issue had never been voiced between the three of them. Sammi knew her mother would disapprove. Eventually, he rejected the idea of buying cigarettes knowing that, even after 22 years of marriage, he'd hate to disappoint his wife. When they'd first got together, all of his friends had told him that he was batting above his average. She was better looking than him and blessed with a more original mind. Those friends were former friends now, carelessly lost, but their original verdict still held true. He was lucky to have her; even without the passion, the impulsiveness, they'd once shared.

He arrived at the office, almost without realising it. He could recall little of the journey, a contemptibly familiar trip of half an hour or so. The dashboard clock confirmed that it had taken a little longer than average that morning, the rain having slowed everything down. There had been fresh flowers on the central-reservation at one point, he remembered that much, and a police sign appealing for witnesses to a fatal accident. Doubtless a motorcyclist. Like the one who used to take Sammi out for a while. How he'd fretted over her safe return each time she'd straddled that

machine; a machine fuelled by high-octane testos-
terone. Perhaps it was that same biker who had died.
That kid had always seemed destined for a tawdry
shrine on the metal grating, separating the east and
westbound carriages of a suburban arterial.

Youth did not seem quite so contemptuous that
morning, though. Not after hearing Sabine. At least,
he assumed that she was young. He would need to
find out about her. He knew he had a meeting
scheduled for 2pm but there was little else to do. Even
since he'd been given his own office, he had rarely
taken advantage of such dead time. It would be
different this morning, though. After the briefest of
'hellos' with colleagues, he closed the door to his
office, uncharacteristically, and immediately googled
Sabine Dean.

First, a video of her performing *Shaken* live on
Spanish television, behind a piano, in front of a few
dozen people. And every single one of them, even the
women, looked as if they had fallen in love with her.
It was the awestruck faces of the audience, rather
than the singer's extreme beauty, which affected him
most. The tobacco content in her voice was even more
pronounced when she sang live. There was an aching
faraway look in her eyes, which verged on the tearful.
His office ceiling whirred around him. He couldn't
even finish watching the four-minute clip. He closed
his eyes, rubbed vigorously at his thinning hair and
called his secretary for a strong cup of tea. Normally
he would have made his own tea, feeling he was
demeaning the secretary by asking her to perform
such a mundane task. Not today, though. He fancied
himself to be in a devil-may-care mood.

Once he'd drunk the tea, he was surfing again. He
discovered that Sabine Dean was 26, a citizen of

America; New York, California, some place out on the Lakes – she was one of life's flitters, nobody could quite place her. She'd played the nightclub circuit, chiefly in New York, for a couple of years before she'd been 'discovered'. He shook his head incredulously that it had taken so long for anyone to acknowledge the blatant obviousness of her star quality. Two years worth of deaf and blind A&R men. She wrote, or co-wrote, all of her own songs and her debut single *Shaken* had been a worldwide hit, her first album due out in a fortnight. In the video for *Shaken*, there were extensive shots of Sabine Dean walking barefoot in a summer dress. And when she walked, it made you want to take up sculpture, just so you might try to capture her curves.

The Googling continued, sporadically, all morning, between occasional work-related banalities. When he found a picture of Sabine Dean, reclining on a sofa in a low-cut top and denim jeans, lips pouting and sadness in her dark Latin eyes, he held his head in his hands, as if to stop the room rotating.

"You're not like this," he told himself. "At least you weren't. Not until now."

And, indeed, he wasn't usually like this at all. The only previous time he'd had a crush on a celebrity, he had been 12 and she had been a Spanish tennis player. At that age, you were allowed to have crushes on celebrities, it was pretty much expected of you. At 45, married with an adult daughter (how he hated to admit the 'adult' bit) and now at the senior end of middle-management, nothing was permitted to take away your breath in this fashion. It was an important part of your duty to keep breathing steadily while others were parting company with their cool. He'd never had real-life crushes either. In fact, he'd never previously considered that they were referred to as 'crushes' because they squeezed the air from your lungs. There had been no extramarital affairs and precious few flirtations. If not exactly happy, he had been lazily content for longer than he could recall, saving any drive he possessed for a career which had been steadily successful, ever since, despite his introverted nature, he'd discovered something of a flair for man-management or for 'mentoring', as the people who refused to use normal language seemed to wish to call it. So steadfast was his career progression, that even his contempt for its jargon had faded. He had truly stepped up to the plate.

But then at midday, sweating at the revelation that Sabine Dean's second single was possibly more hauntingly erotic than her first, he told his secretary to inform colleagues that he would have to call off that afternoon's meeting, due to 'personal issues'. He had never previously taken time away from the office for 'personal issues' and had rarely even had time off sick. So his secretary and colleagues received the news with some surprise but with absolute acceptance, not feeling the need to ask any questions nor even indulge in anything more than the most rudimentary gossip among themselves. The notion that their boss had fallen – plunged headlong – for a young American singer, would have seemed utterly implausible. As he left the office, light-headed and palpitating, he actually smiled at this thought. That he had suddenly developed a mysterious side and that nobody would ever guess.

On his solitary journey in the lift down to reception, he tap-danced on the marble-effect floor, and giggled audibly to himself. He was feeling all the exhilaration of falling in love, without any of the guilt or complications of having an affair. This seemed to him to be the very best of all worlds. And so he drove to the shopping mall, bought himself an iPod and asked the crusty girl behind the counter how to download music, and in particular the first two singles by Sabine Dean. The shop assistant shook her head and smiled with world-weariness, as if she were middle-aged and he the teenager. This was not the first fortysomething bloke to come in asking urgently about Sabine Dean and neither would he be the last.

Next, he wondered which brand of cigarettes Sabine Dean smoked and he took himself to the newsagents. Something American, he imagined, and so he asked for ten Camel Lights, with a guilty head-rush, almost expecting the shop assistant to ask him for ID. Outside of the mall, the most American place he knew of locally, he lit up and felt his head swimming, dragging deeply and imagining himself giving jaw-droppingly good, gravel-voiced karaoke, in the manner of Johnny Cash, to a bar full of young people. He loved the intimacy of the earphones, the clarity of Sabine's voice.

"Honey, I'm shaken,

Shaken by you,

Every time you walk in the room,

Feels like something new,

Shaken by you."

He spent the afternoon in a series of coffee shops, listening to those two songs on a loop, memorising not just the words but each inflection in her voice. This thing, this insane thing, was going to make him happy, he felt. He sprayed his suit with deodorant, washed in the toilets and sucked contentedly on extra strong mints, then drove home to his wife, who didn't notice the slightest thing

* * * * *

His wife had been away at her sister's house for a day and a half before it even occurred to him that she might have been having an affair of her own. A real affair with somebody she had actually met. With no evidence and with no genuine intuition, he swiftly began to accept this possibility as a cast-iron fact and he felt glad for his wife. Why shouldn't she enjoy another man – perhaps younger, better-looking, certainly more attentive and romantic than himself. It would not be as special as the thing he had cultivated with Sabine Dean but it was good for her, all the same. He wouldn't want his wife to leave him, although – and this surprised him – only because of the effect it might have on Sammi, their elderly parents or the gossip it would ignite among their (her) few remaining friends.

That weekend, he'd spent most of his time online, or listening to Sabine Dean's newly-released debut album, always on his earphones, even though he had the house to himself. He'd downloaded the album within minutes of its release, the previous Monday, and he'd been blown away by the melancholy of the lyrics, laced with the dirty sexuality of her voice. Surfing, or rather trawling, the internet for information about her had been an often troubling experience. He'd read what few interviews she had given and felt angered that each journalist – each talentless critic who had been granted time with a woman who was going to end up not as the next Madonna, but the next Monroe – had lingered so long on the alleged negatives. They'd interrogated Sabine Dean on the idea that she had been somehow 'manufactured' – a product of her wealthy father and his alliance with a music mogul. That her song-writing input had been minimal, that her pouting lips had been injected with collagen, her breasts surgically enhanced, and that her very incarnation as a musician had been carefully crafted to satisfy some predictable male fantasy. These accusations had been posted by bloggers and anonymous online types, including, in the worst cases, 'trolls'. And this was how the journalists, with such cowardice, had couched their questions, as if these thoughts could never have crossed their own sympathetic minds on an independent basis.

Bloggers, trolls, messageboards and chatrooms – these words, these notions, had been foreign to him until three weeks ago, yet now they were familiar. He was a member of a chatroom dedicated to Sabine Dean, a follower of her official Twitter and Facebook accounts. Sabine had told her inquisitors that she was aware of the 'haters', and that, yes, such comments had been hurtful at first but that she was merely a shy, introverted girl who was only interested in her music and that she was now determined to ignore any criticism. In this age of technological immediacy, she said, the backlash started before you had even released your first album. She preferred to try and exist in a more innocent age, reflected in the retro sound of her music and fashion. "An age when a star could just be cherished for being a star," he'd told her, in a post to her Twitter account, which he'd hoped that she would see and respond to. Other fans, mostly just kids, had received brief, grateful replies from Sabine Dean and he'd burned with jealousy as he consumed every detail of her timeline.

In one interview, though, she'd confessed – if such a comment need be regarded as a 'confession' – that she had a predilection for older men, but that, no, there was no special person in her life just now and that she simply enjoyed 'hanging out' with other musicians, in whose company she felt safe. This pleased him, that she might find sanctuary in platonic friendships and that she might be protected from the harshness of the media glare. She hadn't asked for any of that intrusion, he knew, she'd wanted only for an audience to enjoy her music. She was shy and introverted, as he had been at her age. She needed a kind, older man, to love her and guide her. Somebody from outside of the unforgiving celebrity world she had recently entered. He would take care of her. Even if he never met her, he'd do all that he could. In her best interests.

Several of the internet comments he'd read, from both women and men, had included the tired old accusation that Sabine was incredibly attractive but that she KNEW it. As if this self-knowledge were some sort of crime. None of these people, he knew, could ever have had a beautiful daughter of their own. For then, you not only hoped but insisted that she must be utterly aware of her own beauty and sexuality, and that the biggest mistake she could ever make would be to underestimate this power. With subtlety, he'd tried to instil this self-awareness into Sammi – but who knew whether she was doing herself justice up in York. Her contact with either parent was negligible now. All he knew was that Sammi was having the time of her life, away from her parents – something he'd wished for and, equally, dreaded.

That weekend, he had become fully embroiled in the malicious, septic world of the online 'community', people who fed off each other's anger, hatred and self-righteousness in an orgy of mutual loathing and petty one-upmanship. First he witnessed, then participated, in debates about the girl he adored. The women who posted comments about Sabine Dean seemed eaten up by bitterness and envy, telling the world that no female could be so talented, beautiful and old-fashioned without being the product of some male Svengali. The men were usually supportive, but often immaturely and fawningly so. This all compelled him, against his better instincts, to intervene on Sabine's behalf.

He'd had to create himself a username for the messageboard and had toyed with something self-deprecating like 'sad dad' but although this amused him, he knew his comments needed to have credence and so he used something close to his own name instead.

"Sabine Dean has astonishing God-given talent and beauty. In a previous age people would simply be able to enjoy that fact, rather than cynically seek to pour scorn on her out of jealousy and bitterness. I was brought up in that previous age, and I'm glad of it. It's clear Sabine would rather have been born a good few years earlier, so as to avoid all of this hatred. I pity you all and hope the anger in you doesn't end up consuming you."

Within minutes the responses to his comment mounted up:

"Fuck you, granddad."

"What are you? Some sort of vicar?"

"Sabine Dean is a capitalist robot whore, constructed for sad old bastards like you. It's you that needs pitying."

"Her dismal music is as fake as her obscene trout lips."

"I only hope you don't have a daughter of your own

who ends up being used as some sick marketing tool."

"I bet you're a paedophile."

"The minds that dreamt up Sabine Dean are the same as those who fantasized about an Aryan master race."

He'd quickly realised that any internet debate, whatever the subject, only had a finite time-span before it descended into accusations of Nazism and/or paedophilia.

The agitation he felt at this abuse soon wore off. It wasn't as if he'd lost all sense of proportion about this thing. After all, he'd been managing to focus on work, to a reasonable degree, and his marriage had been seemingly unaffected; not that there was an awful lot to affect, when he came to think about it. In fact, he'd made love to his wife a little more often than usual. Listening to Sabine's music had evoked something within him. It wasn't as if he'd actually thought of her while having sex. There was just a sense of her presence about him, always. He believed she might have been watching him, which brought out the best in him at home and at work. He'd acted with kindness towards everyone he knew, not that he'd been unkind before. Everything now, though, was heightened. This was what love did to him; much as it had done the last time he experienced it, more than 20 years earlier.

He smoked all weekend long, tossing the butts over the back wall. And he touched himself frequently, without ever coming. He touched himself to the image of Sabine, reclined on that sofa in her denim shorts. Usually he imagined kissing her from her toes to her thighs and then resting his head in her lap, scenting her but never anything more, never spoiling this thing with that wretched sense of emptiness he felt after bringing himself off. So long as he stayed away from the messageboards, Sabine Dean gifted him peace and serenity, like no woman he'd ever met. Only when he heard or watched her sing, with such pain and longing in her voice, did he feel the need to cry. He was shy and introverted too, just as she was. Everybody felt lonely, from time to time, even when they were not alone.

* * * * *

Despite Sabine Dean attaining A-list status on both sides of the Atlantic, he knew she wasn't one to court publicity for publicity's sake. While he was glad of this, knowing that the voracious media would tear her down as soon as they had built her up, it also meant that weeks could pass without any definitive news of her. Even her postings on Twitter and Facebook were few and far between. She no longer responded to any messages from fans, least of all himself, and any social-network updates seemed to have been sent on her behalf, in the perfunctory manner of a record-company minion. At least this meant she would not be listening to those 'haters', which was something of a relief to him.

When news of Sabine Dean did arrive, it came in twos; first the announcement of her UK tour dates, with tickets to go on sale later that week and priority for premium members of the 'Sabine Dean information service'. He'd joined long ago, thanking heaven she hadn't called it a 'fan club'. As well as the arena dates, she would be playing a couple of warm-up gigs at low-key venues. Tickets for these would be available by ballot. So he applied and prayed for the intimacy these small venues would afford them.

The next day, however, messageboards were

flooded with talk of a report in an American magazine that Sabine had become involved with the 'bad boy' Hollywood actor Ryan McKeefe. They'd been pictured together falling out of an L.A nightclub and there had been several other sightings of the couple. He had precious little knowledge of modern-day Hollywood 'bad boys' but it seemed they had moved on little as a species, leaning towards drug-taking, womanising and, of course, 'hell-raising'.

Before he even checked Sabine's Twitter feed, it was crammed with messages warning and admonishing her about this destructive relationship. Naturally, knowing she would be looking out for his guidance, he needed to add to these messages but, in the manner of their relationship, he bade his time and honed his words, wanting to ensure that he would stand out from the crowd. He wasn't naive enough to disbelieve the reports and, though his sense of disappointment had been crushing at first, there was no anger, just an overwhelming desire to guide and to help, now, when she needed it most, more than ever before. Young people would always make their mistakes – it was how they recovered and learned from those errors of judgment which mattered. As a 'mentor' in his professional and private life, he knew this only too well.

And so he wrote: "Forget about the anger, Sabine. Just make sure you make it to Britain so we can cherish you in the flesh. Men will come and go, both good ones and bad, but your music will always be foremost. Never lose sight of that fact and all will be well."

Life continued as normally as it could. He secured tickets for two of Sabine's major London dates and waited for the result of the ballot for her warm-up gigs, knowing these would be over-subscribed but believing that the force which had brought her into his life would continue to make him lucky.

Even when an English tabloid reported that police had been called to a disturbance at a party in McKeefe's apartment, with Sabine present, he clung to the belief that this was some brief rebellious phase, like when Sammi had her nose pierced at 16. His wife had reacted with horror, but he had always maintained a confidence in his daughter's basic decency. And he had been right, at least as far as he was aware. He tried not to imagine Sammi's nights out, or evenings in, at university. She had told her parents that she was planning to return only fleetingly during the three-week Easter holidays and would not be specific about dates.

Mornings, though, were beginning to trouble him. He knew that when he awoke in the London suburbs, it would be approaching midnight in Los Angeles and he grimly imagined that Sabine Dean would be taking cocaine – and please, nothing worse than that – before being fucked, by a drug-crazed Ryan McKeefe. He'd never done anything more serious than smoke a spliff at college himself but he'd heard that cocaine made you insatiably horny. These thoughts made his stomach sick and his cock hard. One morning, soon after arriving at the office, he stood in a toilet cubicle, ejaculated into the bowl and was then unable to hold back tears of regret. He struggled to contain himself in meetings that day, but he thought of his company pension and his companionable wife and knew full-well that he would always manage, somehow.

The celebrity gossip pages were carrying tittle-tattle about Sabine and McKeefe on an almost daily basis now. The actor had had to cancel a day's filming on his new movie after a violent row with the 'sultry songstress', as Sabine Dean was usually described in red-top shorthand. What had felt like no more than disappointment in Sabine, was now becoming a mild crossness. He was annoyed that her dalliance with McKeefe – and he was adamant that this was no more than a brattish 'dalliance' – had become the stuff of tabloid cliche, the kind of story the casual reader would have seen so many times before. Sabine Dean should never be predictable, she was far too talented for that. As the stories became more frequent, he noticed himself beginning to snap at his wife, perhaps no more than he'd tended to do from time to time during their marriage, but it troubled him all the same.

Alone one evening, while his wife told him she was at a new evening class, but was doubtless seeing her lover, he opened up that familiar photo of Sabine Dean in her cut-off jeans and imagined himself on that sofa, putting her across his knee, pulling down her shorts and spanking her with a gentle firmness. She would try to kick a little but would be restrained by the denim around her ankles and his left hand in the small of her back. She would break into sobs at the stinging sensation and the humiliation, but she would then thank him, knowing his cruelty was borne of kindness. That it was all for her own good. But when he fantasized about the redness of her buttocks, he came and felt a miserable shame of his own.

The morning after, he opened an email which told him he had been successful in the ballot for one of Sabine's two London warm-up appearances. In a small bar in Camden, one he had already staked out with an early-evening visit, just in case. For once, he hoped she would never have known nor guessed what he had been imagining the previous night. How could he have wished to punish her when she had illuminated his life so vividly? When she'd made stardust out of sawdust? Where was his gratitude?

He knew that having guaranteed a ticket for such a cosy venue meant he would be certain to catch her eye. Even if they did not speak, he would be convinced that she'd feel blessed that he was looking out for her. He imagined, as in that early Spanish TV clip, that every man in the room would be silently worshipping her. So he would need to buy some clothes for the occasion. Clothes for the stylish middle-aged man and not for the midlife-crisis wannabe teenager. Not an easy balancing act this – but a T-shirt with a slogan, a smart jacket and corduroy trousers, that should do the trick.

In his more reflective moments, he didn't suppose that his admiration for Sabine did an awful lot for his street cred. Indeed, his merely thinking of the phrase 'street cred' meant that he was clearly too old to possess any.

Soon after the release of Sabine's album, though, he had sent a text message to Sammi: "Your old dad's gone and bought the Sabine Dean album! Are you impressed?! x"

A day or so later, his daughter replied: "Oh Daddy Boy, liking Sabine Dean is such a middle-aged male cliche! You do make me laugh! x"

And he'd loved her poking gentle fun at him. Wasn't that exactly what a teenage daughter was supposed to do to her father?

* * * * *

Sammi had arrived home – if indeed their house could still be regarded as her home – completely unannounced on Easter Saturday afternoon, and informed her parents she would be staying for three or four nights. He instantly realised to his horror that the fourth night, the Tuesday after the Easter holidays, was the evening when Sabine Dean would be playing Camden, the first date of her UK tour. He had booked the day off, on the sly, so as to extend his Easter break and had intended to spend much of it browsing around Camden in the manner of a younger or more cosmopolitan man. Still, he assumed that Sammi would not be wanting to spend too much time sitting on the sofa with her parents, as there would surely be old school friends to catch up with. Her parents would probably only see her for a spot of brunch, possibly even lunch, after one of her extended lie-ins. So he resolved, as if there could have been any doubt, to stick with Plan A and attend Sabine's soiree.

When Sammi had breezed into their house, leather-jacketed, with a waft of nicotine and perfume, little had changed about her appearance since a brief visit over Christmas. Yet, he noticed, she was undeniably a woman now. She seemed to hold herself with such worldly confidence, rather than with the embarrassed slouch of a teenager. She had started speaking with deadpan wit, rather than communicating largely through spits and grunts. Though still as cool as a blade, she was conversing with her parents as an equal. Whatever she had found in York, it had allowed her to blossom. And so he wished, privately, that she would shrivel back into her former self. Because she would be gone soon. Gone from this home, for good.

Sammi had responded vaguely to his questions about her university course, her lodgings and her social life and then she had headed to the pub early in the evening. So, alone in the kitchen, early on Sunday morning, he felt embarrassed and self-conscious for having bought Sammi such a childish Easter egg. He'd always bought her Easter eggs, rather than leaving her mother to perform this chore. It had always been his tradition. The eggs were still the same sort of eggs he would have bought her as a toddler. He was still her Daddy Boy, she still his little girl. Was she still his little girl?

By the time his wife had joined him for breakfast, though, he had become all-consumed by potentially devastating internet rumours. There was talk that Sabine Dean had been rushed to hospital in New York after overdosing on heroin at the hotel room she had been sharing with Ryan McKeefe. And this on the evening before she was due to fly to London for her UK tour. While concerned and anxious, he had heard similar lies before, which had spread like internet wildfire and then been swiftly dowsed by Sabine's management company.

Yet when Sammi emerged from her en-suite shower, around midday, three hours had passed, the rumours had become stronger and there had still been no denial. He was beginning to panic over Sabine's well-being, when Sammi strolled in to join him at the dining table in the conservatory, as his wife rustled her up a bacon sandwich and some proper coffee in the kitchen.

Hungover, his daughter was wearing a pink robe and drying her hair with a towel. A bunny-rabbit Easter egg sat on the table as Sammi slumped in the seat opposite her father.

"Hi baby," he offered.

"Hey, Daddy Boy."

"Good night at the pub?"

"Bit of a heavy one," she said, as if she had been enduring serious drinking sessions for decades, "we ended up back at Martha's."

He wondered when girls had become so unashamedly blokeish about their drinking, but instead of wondering this out loud, he merely asked how Martha was.

"She's bored with life, bored with this place, wished she had accepted that offer at Aberystwyth now. Middle of nowhere though, isn't it, Aberystwyth? Even for Wales."

Sammi shook out her dark, damp hair, with something approaching supermodel attitude and before Martha could be discussed any further, she became engrossed in her mobile phone.

"Hey, d'ya hear about your heart-throb?"

"Heart-throb?"

"Sabine Dean."

"She's hardly a heart-throb, baby, I just enjoy her music that's all."

"Yeah, right, well doesn't sound like there's going to be much more music."

"What do you mean? What have you heard?" he asked, unable to disguise his sense of dread.

"According to Twitter, she's brown bread."

"No, that can't be true."

"Sounds like it's just been confirmed."

For the first time that day, sunshine had broken out against the conservatory windows. It felt uncomfortably hot. The room seemed to blur. He stood as if to open the patio door but his legs felt incapable of supporting him. This was not the way he should have heard. Not while in the company of his wife, not through the blasé words of his attitudinal daughter and certainly not by means of Cockney rhyming slang. Since when had Sammi started using rhyming slang?

He took his Blackberry from his trouser pocket and a red light was blinking, indicating an internet alert he had set up for Sabine Dean's name. The BBC was reporting breaking news, and Sammi read out the newsflash from her Twitter feed, just as his own disbelieving eyes were scanning across the same statement.

"Here y'are," said Sammi. "The American singer Sabine Dean was pronounced dead on arrival at a New York hospital after a suspected drug overdose, according to police sources. She was twenty-seven."

"My God," he said, grinding his fingers into his forehead, while conscious of trying to appear like nothing more than a casual fan.

So this was how it would end, then. No Camden. They would never meet. Never even breathe the same air in the same room. She was gone. Sabine Dean's body would be lying on a mortuary slab. Die young and leave a beautiful corpse, they said.

"She was shagging that actor McKeefe, wasn't she?" said Sammi. "Proper wrong 'un, him. Mind you, fair play to her, he is really hot."

"Mind your language, darling," said his wife, carrying in the cafetiere.

"Sorry, mother," Sammi chirruped, affecting an upper-class accent. "They're a potty-mouthed bunch in those shared student houses, you know, I must have become infected with their dreaded lurgy."

"Is McKeefe dead too?" he asked his daughter, hopefully. He was aware of the pressure points in his wrists, the veins straining, his blood almost literally seeming to boil at the mention of the actor's name and his own sweet daughter's attraction to such lowlife.

184

"No, don't think so. Did you hear that, Mum? That singer Sabine Dean's died of a drug overdose."

"No. Oh, I think your dad quite liked her, didn't you, love?"

Why did she speak of Sabine in the past tense? Sabine would never be in the past tense. Her music would always be there. He tried, desperately, to maintain a look of outward calm. He knew his wife had never seen him become emotional about the death of a celebrity. Indeed, he had often asked her how she could shed tears over the passing of someone she had never met.

"Yes, yes, darling, she has a lovely voice, HAD a lovely voice," he said, his voice breaking up. "I'm sorry I think I'm coming down with a bug. Flu or something. I need some fresh air."

"Yes, maybe you should pop outside, it's a lovely, fresh spring day out there."

Before he could move, Sammi averted her gaze from her phone and piped up again.

"Oh yeah, twenty-seven she was. I'd forgotten that thing about twenty-seven. People are saying it on Twitter. The Twenty-Seven Club!"

"What about twenty-seven?" asked her mother.

Her father, his head in his hands, feigning illness, already knew the answer.

"They were all twenty-seven, all the rock stars who died young. Kurt Cobain, twenty-seven; Amy Winehouse, twenty-seven; Jimi Hendrix, twenty-seven; Jim Morrison, twenty-seven; Janis Joplin ..."

"Well, at least all this should make you less likely to do drugs up in York," said her mother. "Illegal ones at least."

And with a shake of the head, she shuffled back into the kitchen to serve up Sammi's breakfast. The smell of the frying bacon and the coffee, was becoming overpowering. He began to feel nauseous.

"How predictable, though. What a cliché, dying at twenty-seven!" said Sammi, moving up a gear as the caffeine surged inside her.

He shot a fierce look at his daughter, through reddened eyes, but she barely seemed to notice his anger, before returning to her Twitter feed, devouring scores of flippant messages about the young woman whose death had been announced barely five minutes earlier. The woman her father worshipped and adored.

This was how deaths were now marked – either by fanatical outpourings of grief or by waspish comments buzzing between smartphones across the globe. No time now for quiet contemplation or the respectful removal of hats. By the time Sabine Dean was lifted into her hearse, she would be old news. They would all be on to the next thing. Sabine would no longer even be 'trending worldwide'.

"Oh, ouch," said Sammi, giggling. "Someone's tweeted 'how can a manufactured robot singer actually die?' Bitchy, eh?"

He clenched his fist, wishing to hammer it down on the Easter bunny egg, which sat on the table between them, unwrapped, unmentioned, seemingly unnoticed by Sammi. He wished to crush the cardboard, tinfoil and milk chocolate and everything it had symbolised when he had bought it for her. Instead, though, he bit deeply into the skin on his own forefinger and felt glad to feel the pain.

12

GREENWICH MEAN TIME

I should keep a diary. Not a warts-and-all confessional. Who'd want to read about my verrucas when I'm gone? No, just a pocket diary to record the basic facts of where my life's going and where it's been. I might have had a more successful career or retained more friends had I not double-booked myself so often or failed to send so many birthday cards. In fact, I sleep so heavily that if it wasn't for my old-school alarm clock – the cartoon variety, with clanging bells – I doubt if I'd often get up in the morning.

And, looking retrospectively, who knows when I might need a genuine alibi? A slim journal available for £5.99 from WH Smith might just spare me a life sentence for a murder I did not commit, some day.

I'm not especially chaotic and disorganised, nor particularly free-spirited and Que Sera, Sera about things. It's just that I always feared my diary would possess too many blank rectangles. What diary-carriers refer to as 'windows', while always hinting that these must, by definition, be few and far between.

The devil is in the detail, you see. Being aware of the date of St Patrick's Day might prove crucial when romancing some Irish woman with distance in her eyes and wildness in her heart. Likewise, the staging of Yom

Kippur, when it came to charming some ample-breasted Jewish girl.

You're right, of course, this nagging diary issue hasn't been brought on by fears for my career, friends, family or even the potential for wrongful conviction. It's basically about women. And one woman in particular. Not that I'm a totalitarian when it comes to these things. The romcom concept of 'The One' was invented to appease insecure women, I'm certain of that. Don't even mention the word 'soulmate' to me. I'm always wary of two words becoming one, it always seems a bit Germanic, for starters. So no, I do not believe that Juliet Squires was put on this Earth to be my spiritual reflection. I'm from Yorkshire, which is not such a bold statement as it was among my father's generation, perhaps, but it's still bloody Yorkshire.

I have happily visited the spa sections of hotels but 'relaxation techniques' make me violent. I am capable of articulating my emotions after a few pints of beer, but men who use moisturiser make me feel deeply uneasy. I have A levels and an above average annual salary but I like gravy on my chip shop chips. This is just a sketch, you understand. I'm sketching for you here. In case you want to pigeon-hole me – and I'm not one of those people who go around saying 'don't pigeon-hole me' either. I'm not unreconstructed but we've all got roots and there's only so far they'll stretch.

Likewise, Juliet Squires was named after her parents' favourite fictional character – but we are talking Juliet Bravo, here, not Capulet. She was from Yorkshire too. Inspector Kate Longford on the portable, three bars on the electric fire, a faint whiff of damp vegetables in the air, this was where she hailed from. At least, I'm assuming. I never met her parents, let alone discussed the conception of their daughter.

A dozen years ago, we both found ourselves marooned in the same London suburb. Exiles gravitate towards one another. No gravy in the chip shops down here. No day-trips to Whitby harbour. And the locals around here, their default setting is 'angry' rather than merely 'miserable', like in the North. A frown is so much more homely than a scowl, don't you think?

Well, I'm still here but Juliet's long gone. It's not like I'm generally prone to self-pity, or uneasy with my own company. The voice in my head is a Yorkshireman too. Sceptical, realistic, not allowing myself to get too carried away. There's no melodrama. And it is not as if there haven't been other women since Juliet. Longer relationships, which to friends and acquaintances, might have appeared more meaningful. No, if I'd been especially bothered about having just anybody to spend my life with then I wouldn't be alone on this or any other evening.

It is only really on Sunday evenings that I tend to start pining for Juliet. When I'm strolling out to the cashpoint and the minimarket for my cigarettes. I ask the dumpy pacamacked Turkish woman for ten, as if I might quit tomorrow. Then I ask her for a packet with a different health warning, the one about low sperm count or not making children inhale cyanide, anything except this one; the bloke with the cancerous growth wrapped round his neck, like Bib Fortuna from Return of the Jedi. But the Turkish woman is too busy Facebooking on her laptop to comprehend me. This is the 21st century. A cousin in Ankara wants a recipe for honey almond cake. Eat sweetly and speak sweetly, say the Turks. So later, I will slip a small passport-sized photo of my niece into the polythene casing around my cigarette packet, so as to obscure the man who wears his tumour like a scarf. I don't want to ponder death on a Sunday night. Not a death as gruesome and self-inflicted as that, at any case.

Life, though, is all about having somebody to share a Sunday evening with. Somebody to make you forget about the length of the week that's lying in wait for you. Any other time of the week just seems to fill itself, one way or another. It's a fair cop, though, my one indulgence is pitying myself on a Sunday evening. Ever since that last Sunday in March, 2002.

Diary or no diary, it's not as though I hadn't been warned. Since well before we'd got to the stage of spending Sunday evenings together, Juliet had spoken with great certainty about her delayed 'gap year'. Her and her mate Sophie from back home. South America rather than Asia and Australia. This made her trip the subject of envy for me, as well as melancholy. Machu Picchu and Galapagos turtles, the carnival and the Pampas. The itinerary always sounded like a series of taunts. It made me terse with her and hateful of myself.

Then, six weeks before the off, Sophie bottles it. Her mum is ill. But her mum is always ill. Her job's looking promising. But wasn't this all about escaping from work? A long-term fuck-buddy has suddenly become a 'soulmate'. Ah, so that'll be it then. She'd always been man-hungry had Sophie (according to Juliet, I never met Sophie). Initially, my heart soars. Then I suggest that maybe I should take the trip with Juliet. Notice handed to the boss and caution tossed to the wind.

But I've never been one to seize the hour. Not impulsive, never been impulsive, as much as I'd love to be. That and enigmatic. I've always wished I could, just once, be described as 'enigmatic'. So a while later, I told Juliet that I couldn't join her and she didn't try too hard to change my mind, now I come to think about it. Anyway, the Yorkshireman inside my head was adamant that she wouldn't go to South America alone. Not for a whole year, anyway. She had a certain freedom of spirit, sure, but she'd maybe just shorten the trip to a month or six weeks, maybe do a deal with her boss, then head back to her old job, the Monday morning after a Sunday evening in bed with me and a chicken jalfrezi. That's what I believed.

If Juliet Squires, as elegant as the letters of her name appear when written in 12-point Calibri (Body), had genuinely been my one true love, then perhaps I'd never have underestimated the determination in her soul. Because she left her job on the last Thursday in March, held leaving drinks with friends and colleagues in London on the Friday, then spent Saturday at my flat, which had been our mutual home for just a fortnight, since she'd vacated her own rented apartment. We made love, packed bags, ticked off checklists, and the girl was still intransigent in her desire to do this thing before she was 30, in the spirit of the age. And if she was going away for a whole year – three times as long as our relationship had been considered by society as 'serious' – then neither of us was naive enough to expect the other one to wait. Though in hindsight she, at least, would have been right to do so.

It was only on that last Saturday evening when I became certain she was actually going to go through with it. The short minicab ride, from my flat in the Heathrow flightpath, had been booked. I'd have given her a lift, of course, but she claimed that an airport farewell was more than she could bear. This, in itself, seemed like an admission that the emotion would sting her, make her doubt. It had given me some selfish satisfaction. Made me believe that perhaps I had meant enough for her to look me up on her return.

So we went to bed early on the Saturday night, knowing her alarm was set for 6am, her cab for 6.45am, her flight at 9am. A no-nonsense schedule for a no-nonsense girl. I was saddened, though, when she fell asleep so soon after we'd made love that final time. Even though she generally would have done, on any other night. Even though this had always been billed as a butterfly romance with a finite lifespan, thanks to Sugarloaf Mountain, Caracas and the Inca Trail. Even though we'd drunk a bottle of Mateus Rosé apiece that night, not because we couldn't afford a better bottle of wine, just because we both loved Mateus Rosé. A shared guilty pleasure, more readily available in the London suburbs than gravy on your chips.

Yet Juliet's sleep was restless, mine non-existent, and around about midnight I gripped her tight, my fingernails in her shoulder blades, my tear-salt on her lips, and I told her, "baby, I'll come with you, I'll buy a ticket at the airport." She sounded unconvinced by my suggestion, underestimating me, as I'd underestimated her, because, in the first and only truly impulsive moment of my life, I set my old alarm clock for 6am. Either I'd persuade Juliet to stay or I'd buy a ticket for the Rio flight on my credit card and to hell with it all. And, resolved to this, the Mateus Rosé carried me away to sleep. How enigmatic they would think me, my work colleagues, when I'd phone them from Copacabana Beach and tell them to stick their job.

I think I was still dreaming of the sand, when my alarm clock started clattering furiously and I was left staring at a note on her pillow, killing all impulse:

"Baby, you were sleeping so deeply and I didn't want to wake you. I don't really do goodbyes, I am from Yorkshire after all! I'm glad your coffee is pure, strong Brazilian, especially after losing that hour. x"

Juliet hadn't mentioned it and I soon supposed that this may have been deliberate. But you cannot seize the hour, when the hour has been lost. The last Sunday in March. British Summer Time begins.

And she kept a diary, you see.

13

ALL OUR BONFIRES

Part One: Will

I can tell that Scott is listening to Springsteen on his iPod again. He's been having a real Springsteen phase lately. Never a good sign. All graduation gowns, Harley-Davidsons and sentimentality. It'll be *Fast Car* by Tracy Chapman next, you mark my words. Then there'll be trouble.

One of Scott's famous playlists is probably called 'Songs about trying to escape small town America (for miserable commutes on a drizzly day)'.

We're from a London suburb with a dog track, a knock-off market and an appetite for wanton violence. We've got enough things of our own to want to escape from, without pretending we need to escape from American things. I've told him this but he never listens. Some people think I'm the stubborn, opinion-ated one but I swear he never listens to a word I say.

The worry for me is that Scott regresses, gets disillusioned with his job, jacks it in, gets ill again and stops going out of the flat, like he did seven or eight years ago.

The only problem for me was that I hated doing the shopping. One thing he's always tended to do is the shopping and, apart from one incident where he bought cheap coffee and tipped it into a proper coffee jar, as if I wasn't going to realise, he does a pretty good job of it.

Then there was the fact that I felt like I could never bring a bird home. Or if I did, it was always, "Who's the deadbeat on the sofa?" - "That's Scotty, my flatmate, he's agoraphobic" – "What does that mean? He's scared of getting into a fight?" – "No it means he's scared of pretty much anything outside these four walls." Which simply wasn't conducive to womanising, not by any stretch of the imagination.

So I said, "Scotty, go and see a shrink or I'll evict you." It was pretty much as blatant as that. When he's had a few to drink these days he sometimes starts giving it, "You saved my life back then, you were cruel to be kind, but you shook me out of it and got me back on my feet. Thanks mate." He forgets how it actually was and, like I said, he sentimentalises, but I can assure you I was acting entirely out of self-interest.

 And it wasn't like he just did what I said, straight off. First he argued the toss about whether I could, legally, evict him. Which, technically, I probably couldn't have done.

Then he started saying, "What's the point in going to see a shrink anyway? I have a good relationship with my parents. Okay, I USED to have a good relationship with my parents. I had a happy childhood. I played golf with my dad, I talked to my mum, those kind of things."

And I said: "It's not all to do with your childhood, Scotty, that's a fallacy. That's just one branch of psychology. Freud or something."

"Freud is the fucking FATHER of psychology," he said, because he could be a smartarse, even when he was ill. "That's like saying only part of The Bible is to do with God. And what do you know about psychology anyway?" – because he can be gobby, too. Hostile.

"I fucked a shrink once," I told him. "She came like a train," I digressed. And, boy, she did, as it happens. "Analyse that, you bitch," I told her. And funnily enough she just LOVED dirty talk. I think they're all a bit fucked in the head, that lot, otherwise they would never have ended up working in mental health in the first place.

Anyway, I told Scott: "When me and the shrink were having a cigarette afterwards, I said, "Hey, actually, could you, y'know, give me a session, like, on the couch, kind of thing?" She said: "Here's the deal, you write a song about me and I'll psychoanalyse you." But, of course, I never could ..."

"You never could write lyrics," Scotty says, then he twigged, "Uh, I think I remember this, was it a couple of years ago when you had that riff and you said 'fit some words around this – but the song has got to be called *Head Shrink Bitch On Heat*?"

"Yeah."

"And you only actually said that to me because you wanted to boast that you had shagged a psychiatrist, while pretending to be subtle about it."

So this was Scotty, circa 2002. You tried to help the bloke and you were branded an egomaniac.

And let's face it, for all his flair for words, his turn of phrase, his reading of 'important' novels, the last girl Scott fell in love with was a lapdancer from Ulster. He told her he was something of a lyricist and she told him that she had written a novel about growing up during The Troubles but, get this, it was a HUMOROUS book about The Troubles! I swear it.

So when she'd failed to return his calls, Scotty's moping about in the flat and he says, with a straight face: 'The next time I see her, she'll be on Newsnight, that lapdancer bird. Or, even worse, the Late Review. She'll have been shortlisted for the Booker Prize or The Nobel fucking Peace Prize'.

He has to talk up this lapdancer as if she's James Joyce in a G-string. So do you think that if HE had shagged a psychiatrist, he would have kept quiet about it? A lapdancer can't just be a lapdancer, with Scott. No, she has to be an intellectual who's experimenting with the Burlesque or some such bollocks. This is his problem with women, always has been. He puts them on a pedestal.

Since he got over his agoraphobia thing – if it even WAS agoraphobia and not just a lengthy bout of moodiness – he became a terrible hypochondriac, which was bad enough in itself, but the last time he was serious with a woman, this Samantha bird, well Scott suffered hypochondria BY PROXY! Every time she said she had anything wrong with her, he started imagining she had cancer, urging her to go to the doctors all the time. The girl started getting seriously freaked about it all. She told me about it, one night, when she came round to the flat and he was out uptown with work people. Soon she stopped telling him about it, even if she just had a cold or a period pain. Eventually she basically stopped talking to him at all. Then she left him. I shagged her, that night, Samantha. Scotty doesn't know that, actually. She was a bit of a cold fish, though, I found, so there probably was something wrong with her, to be fair to him.

In fact, in all the years I've known him, the only time Scotty has truly lightened up is when he was on stage. He would lose himself, and I have to admit, he should have been some kind of superstar. He still could be, even at his age, if he hadn't given up the ghost and tried to get a 'proper' career. He couldn't exactly SING but I've never known anyone to work an audience so well, never known anyone with such energy, with such stage presence. Everyone said so. He was something else. He was certainly somebody else, not the regular Scott Binks you see dossing round this flat. And this is one of the main reasons why we should be playing again, find a bass player, put on a few gigs. Who knows, maybe we could still have another crack at it. We came pretty close to getting signed once, around about '95, so if he could just rediscover that energy, who knows?

It's a long shot, looking at him these days. It's the commuting, the breakfast-on-the-go and the pay-as-you-earn, the drinks after work with the boys, the water cooler moments with the girls. In the winter, he never sees daylight. His skin looks grey. And the very idea of going lapdancing. I mean, that's just giving up, isn't it? Admitting that you are incapable of actually pulling an attractive bird without paying for her.

He's middle-aged before his time. It's not just Springsteen, who, to be fair, I actually rate. He's started listening to Dire Straits. Just the other night, he provoked the most almighty row. He's got his iPod on, playing furious air guitar, and he suddenly takes out one earpiece and says: "The guitar solo in *Sultans of Swing* is even better than the piano solo in *My Baby Just Cares For Me*."

Now he knows this is 'hello Mr Bull, meet my friend the red rag' kind of stuff. In fact, if I'd had a drink in my hand, I'd have glassed him, rather than waste my breath arguing about it. He knows I think Nina Simone is a goddess.

"What the fuck are you talking about, Scotty?"

"I know you won't agree but that's just on the basis

that it's unfashionable to like Dire Straits, but if you actually LISTENED to *Sultans of Swing*, you'd appreciate that it's just as good, technically."

He likes to suggest that I am a music snob. As if I actively avoid listening to stuff that I secretly like, just to appear sophisticated. When, in fact, I simply happen to have a better taste in music than he does. Better taste all round, in all honesty.

"You can't even begin to argue that," I said. "It's not even in the same post code as that piano solo."

"That's an Americanism," he says, all smug, because using Americanisms in conversation has always been a criminal offence in this flat, but, of course, he's got carried away and failed to engage his brain, as usual, which is why he never wins an argument.

"What's an Americanism?"

"In the same postcode!"

"It is not a fucking Americanism, they don't even say 'postcode' in America."

His face drops. He knows I'm right.

"What do they say in America instead of postcode? What do they say, punk?"

He knows this is an ironic use of 'punk' so even he doesn't try to argue that one.

"Zipcode," he says, after a long pause.

"Zipcode. Now if I'd said 'not in the same ballpark', you'd have had an argument. Case dismissed, Scotty, you can't even get basic facts right, so you are not even fit to put Nina in the dock."

"'Case dismissed' is an Americanism. They only say that in American courtroom dramas. Can you imagine an Old Bailey judge saying 'case dismissed'? It wouldn't happen."

This is a tactic of his when he is losing an argument,

changing the subject so he can score a petty point or two.

"I am simply asking you to listen to *Sultans of Swing* and tell me the guitar solo is not amazing."

"You're middle-aged already, Scotty, I never thought I'd see the day."

"I'll accept that it's a guilty pleasure to like a bit of Dire Straits, you can have that, but you have to listen to it and weight it up."

"I can assure you that all my guilty pleasures are pleasures for which I could actually be found guilty in a court of law. If this Dire Straits argument went to a court of law, well it wouldn't even GET to court. It wouldn't get past the CPS – I won't say District Attorney – because it would be a waste of public funds."

But this was not a court of law – on either side of the Atlantic. We were two sad wasters sitting in a flat.

"Listen to *Sultans of Swing*."

Needless to say, I wouldn't.

To shut out his noise, I put on my own iPod. This was our mutually preferred method of finding a bit of space, these days. My playlists may not be as numerous or as convoluted as Scott's but I would agree with him that the iPod is the most significant technological leap forward since we moved into this place.

We had thought that cable TV would revolutionise our lives, by ending any threat of boredom. But we have 600 channels to choose from now and we still can't find much worth watching. We find ourselves yearning for the days when we first moved in. Natalie Imbruglia in her school uniform in Neighbours. Don't worry, Natalie was legal then, even if Beth, her character, might not have been. And we wouldn't have been much older than her, anyway. Fuck, we've been living here a long time. Seventeen years. They doff their caps to married couples who last that long, these days, don't they?

Yes, it's sad that iPods have rendered the good old-fashioned compilation tape obsolete. And they have done no favours to your cracking pub with the quality jukebox either. What's the value of a really good jukebox when everybody has their own perfect jukebox tucked in their inside pocket? But that little machine has certainly filled up many empty hours. It's stopped me from murdering Scotty Binks a few times, that's for sure.

* * * * *

Part Two: Scott

It must have been fifteen years since I almost became a rock star. And, each day, I am still finding new ways in which to regret the word 'almost'.

Will and I moved into this flat in 1995, the year Pulp released *Different Class*. One of the few things we've ever agreed upon, me and Will, is that Jarvis Cocker was writing about us. *Common People* was our anthem.

"Rent a flat above a shop/cut your hair and get a job/smoke some fags and play some pool/pretend you never went to school ..."

So we rented a flat above a shop. Not your average grocery store or takeaway joint, admittedly. An undertaker's. *Up Above The Corpse Lock-Up*, that was one of our songs. The rent was lower than it would have been for a flat above a regular shop, apparently. The landlord clearly didn't know that if you spent much of your time trying to pull Goth girls, this macabre setting was actually a selling point rather than a drawback. And at least there were no neighbours able to complain about the noise of our song-writing sessions, frequent parties and less frequent sexual conquests.

Of all our mates, we were the first to move out of home. Will had inherited a bit of cash and insisted that having our own space was the only way we'd ever make a go of our band, The Crack Babies. It seemed as though everyone was in a band back then. And, so, when we started renting our own place, friends from other bands, and friends of theirs from other bands, would often call round for a drink and a smoke and a jam. These were heady days. The freedom and independence were intoxicating, we were starting to gig regularly and we were developing something of a following. Will always could play a guitar like an angel played a harp. I could write lyrics, sing a little and, much to my own surprise, it turned out that I actually BELONGED centre-stage with a mic at my mouth. On stage, when the lights went down, I was no longer a shy, inhibited schoolboy frightened to even talk to whichever girl I happened to be in love with at the time. I was no longer the son of my introverted, downtrodden father, destined for a similar tongue-tied, desk-bound life to him. I was no longer ignored. No longer treated with disdain or contempt. For the one and only time in my life, I shone. Girls loved me. Even actual women loved me. When I screamed out our punk-rock cover version of Whitney Houston's *The Greatest Love Of All* I'm not even sure I was being all that ironic about the merits of learning to love one's self. Fronting a band was the only thing in life I've ever been really, truly good at.

Over the next year or two Will and me, Steve the

bass player and Micky the drummer went as far as the big side of small-time. In fact, we were verging on the small side of big-time when the whole thing imploded. Just as the record company A&R men were beginning to circle us, Steve had a major drug episode and Micky was arrested for, and eventually convicted of, printing forged banknotes.

The band never really took off again after that, despite a couple of aborted attempts. The moment seemed to have passed. Will never stopped gigging, with his father's pub band and eventually, with some success, on a venture of his own. He only ever wanted to play the guitar. I envied him that simply performing for a dozen or so people in a pub, could make him content. For me, it was all-out rock 'n' roll stardom or nothing. For several years I didn't even pick up my guitar in the flat. I cut my hair and got a proper job. As far as I was concerned, the forces of reality had quelled us, they had pissed on all our bonfires.

And yet somehow, a decade and a half later, we'd never moved on. What should have been a short-term flat-share arrangement seems to have morphed into a partnership for life. Women came and went, for both of us, though more so for Will. And yet neither of us were ever inclined to actually, officially, move out of the flat above the funeral director's.

I got ill and then better again, thanks to a major kick up the arse from Will, although he'd hate to take any credit for that. Will has simply never grown up. He treats women the same now as he did when he was a horny teenager. Peter Pan Handle, I call him. The older he's got and the more ridiculous our situation may have appeared from the outside, the more self-righteous and pig-headed he has become.

Nobody who has existed in relative poverty for so

long – who has lived in a poky flat above an undertakers and survived almost exclusively on Wimpy burgers, Pringles, Jack Daniel's and Marlboro reds for the best part of two decades – has any right to be as snobbish as Will.

And yet Will is snobbish about music, he is snobbish about beer, he is snobbish about coffee, he is snobbish about clothes, despite having barely bought any since the 1990s, he is snobbish about women, even though he's not had too many of those lately, either.

In an England where inverted snobbery is the new snobbery, Will Wilcox is a good old-fashioned un-inverted snob. Without even having the breeding. There's always been a certain minor showbiz quality about his family, I guess, but in essence he is Estuary white trash just as much as I am. Will's grandfather, Bill, was a puppeteer who had written and starred in a 1960s children's TV programme called *Rock 'N' Roll Fox* about the Elvis Presley of the vermin kingdom. It had a mercifully short run but excerpts have recently turned up on YouTube, much to Will's delight. Then Will's father, Bill's son Willie, was the drummer in The Smut, one-hit wonders of the '70s with the ludicrous *Sweet Sally Sugar*, still a favourite with your more chimp-like wedding DJs.

Now, the vast majority of our evenings are spent at the flat, in one another's company. We barely even get out to The Golden Goose any more. Our favourite boozer, our only boozer, is a bus or taxi-ride away in the town centre. The Wimpy across the road is about as adventurous as we usually get.

Will's Wimpy diet is, however, beginning to take its toll on his waistline, especially since a disastrous attempt at giving up smoking, which had wrecked his last semi-serious relationship with a woman about a year ago. Poor girl, Julia. It was one thing going out with a misogynist. Another thing going out with a misogynist suffering from nicotine withdrawal.

So we were left alone to bicker and bitch and whinge and snigger. Evenings were often spent flicking aimlessly through hundreds of cable channels playing our favourite parlour game 'murder the TV personality in the most appropriate fashion' – this had begun back in the early '90s when Will had suggested a computerised strain of myxomatosis was needed to wipe out Jive Bunny.

Over the years we had found myriad ways of killing time, murdering time, torturing time, wiring up time's testicles with electrodes and making time scream for mercy.

There had been evenings spent compiling spoof Glastonbury bills, full of imaginary bands with comedy names. Should Lesbian Shoe Factory headline the main stage on the Saturday night or what about The Welsh Daleks? And let's not forget Chocolate Speedway and The Dressdown Fridays.

Then there were large swathes of time spent debating which was the best cheese snack. This came from my impassioned love of Cheeselets and Will's insistence that they were evil, as moreish as heroin, the Class A of nibbles. In turn, he would swear by those card-suit snacks – cheese hearts, diamonds, spades and clubs. Always supermarket own-brand, never properly marketed or advertised, criminally under-rated, he insisted. Then Mini Cheddars, Wotsits, cheese footballs, cheese straws. Occasionally these conversations sparked frenzied runs to the Seven-Eleven, for gluttonous cheese-snack eat-offs, quarter-finals, semi-finals, finals. And these always ended up in petty, vituperative rows.

Will's passion for bar snacks knew few bounds. Once, when barred from the Golden Goose for persistent petulance, he asked a girlfriend whether she would strip to her underwear and pin packets of peanuts to her body so as to effectively recreate the Big D board from behind the bar at the pub. The girl seriously considered this request, before rejecting him on a technicality. The adhesive which would have been required might aggravate her eczema, I seem to recall.

And of course there were the fractious debates about which of the nineteen naked women on the cover of Hendrix's *Electric Ladyland* we'd most like to have sex with. The French-looking girl with pert tits on the far right usually got my vote. Will veered between the black girl, the skinny one with the tan at the back, the girl at the front showing a piece of arse or even the big old Dawn French lookalike.

And then, most tragically of all, there were evenings spent pretending to interview each other for music magazines or broadsheet arts sections. This one was always Will's idea. In fact, I was always the interviewer and he the interviewee. During one of these sessions, he once imagined that he'd been arrested and that his police mugshot had turned up on T-shirts. And he claimed he had one of those car bumper stickers that read 'My Other Car's A Porsche' on the back of his Ferrari. I've refused to join in on that one in recent years. It really would be too tragic.

On less sociable evenings we listened individually to our iPods, I am trying to compile playlists for every conceivable mood and eventuality. It started off with playlists entitled 'Happy', 'Grumpy', 'Sleepy', 'Bashful' and 'Dopey'. I couldn't think of any particularly sneezy songs, to be honest. Now there's a 'Saturday night' list, a 'Sunday morning' list, a 'Monday morning commute' list, a 'Friday afternoon commute' list. A 'Tuesday playlist' full of quirky shit from years ago. Will hates all this. Because he secretly wishes he'd had the idea himself. It would have killed so much time for him during the long days he spends around this flat doing God knows what.

* * * * *

Part three: Will and Scott

"Do you think that two straight men could form a civil partnership?" asked Scott.

"You what?"

"You know, like a gay wedding but between two straight men?"

"What do you mean?"

"Well, I've decided to join my company pension scheme ..."

"As if you'll live to be retirement age."

"Fuck's sake, Will ..."

Will knew Scotty tended to fret about his health, especially since his 'black dog days' years before.

"Anyway, what's that got to do with gay weddings?"

"Well, when you fill out the pension forms, you have to nominate a beneficiary for the 'death in service' thing."

Scott could see Will's eyes glazing over. Any conversation purporting to regular full-time employment was anathema.

"I never thought I would hear you discussing nominating beneficiaries for a pension scheme ..."

"Well, who should I nominate? My parents don't need the money, I haven't seen my brother since that night we supported Sister Psychotic in 1995 and there aren't exactly any women beating down my door these days."

"That stripper from Londonderry must have lost your number, that's all I can say."

"Go fuck yourself, Will."

"So you're saying that I am your next of kin."

"Depressing, I know, but not far from the truth – and if I wasn't pretty convinced that you would gladly murder me for the sake of a meagre inheritance ..."

"You'd nominate me!"

And there they were, like a married couple of a certain generation, their grandparents' generation. A generation in which couples stayed together, no matter what. Because that was what people did. Because they didn't really know anything different. Because they doubted whether anybody else would actually want them.

"If we went on *Mr and Mrs*, we'd piss it," said Scott, "Only when they brought back *Mr and Mrs*, it had to be *All Star Mr & Mrs* of course."

"I know, Joe Public can't go on quiz shows any more. Except for daytime stuff. It's a fucking outrage."

"Yeah, but then there's always talent shows ..."

"Don't fucking start, Scotty."

He knew, of course, that Scott was about to start. Like a nagging wife, whose husband had strayed once, many years ago, and who never let him forget about it, he was trying to provoke a discussion about Will's appearance on *Stars In Their Eyes* – shortly after the implosion of the original Crack Babies.

"Remember when you used to whinge on about how difficult it was for us 'proper' bands to get gigs because all the venues were filled up with tribute acts?"

Will was trying desperately hard not to bite.

"And then, as if by magic, there you were: Tonight, Matthew, I'm going to be Jarvis Cocker.

"At least I fucking did something for once in my life. For once in our lives."

And that fact really did hurt Scott. Served him right.

"The nearest either of us got to 'making it' was when you pretended to be somebody else," he said.

And when they stopped to think about it, this truth injured them both.

"We've got to sort out that 'Bass Player Wanted' ad," said Will.

"You're only saying that cos nobody wants to book you any more – although you're probably getting too fat for all that Jarvis stuff."

Will had made a tidy living from gigging as 'Jarvis Mocker', chiefly on the university circuit. Yet the bookings had dried up recently. He had regarded the demise of Pulp and Cocker's descent into arthouse obscurity as a personal slight upon himself. Rock stars never considered the tribute acts they'd inspired. Struggling musicians who were basically their dependents.

"Okay so you're 36 and I'm 37," said Will. "The Rolling Stones are practically a hundred but people still watch them. There's no reason why we should be too old."

"All we need is one great album. Bands only ever make one great album nowadays."

"Yeah, well it's obvious why. The first album is always a load of songs about trying to get laid – full of rage and frustration and sardonic pessimism. If the first album is a great album, then the second album is always a load of songs about actually getting laid. Rock lyricists have no imagination, they just write about what they know. And songs about trying and failing to

209

get laid are far better than songs about getting laid. Ordinary people can only identify with failure and misery. Hope, maybe, but mainly failure and misery."

"Yeah, I can identify with those."

"As could any 36-year-old man who's thinking of nominating his flatmate as his death-in-service beneficiary."

Yet Scott had been thinking, scheming, concocting, waiting to run his little brainwave past Will but approaching the subject with great trepidation.

"Yeah but listen, we know we've got one great album in us. We've already got a great album written. It'd just be a case of sorting the wheat from the chaff. We've got twenty years' worth of songs. Great music isn't enough, though, what we need is a scam, a ruse, a publicity stunt to get us noticed."

"A publicity stunt?"

"Well, this is why I was asking you about whether two straight men could form a civil partnership."

"You want us to form a civil partnership? Jesus, you've really lost it this time."

"Listen to me for a minute. Let's face it, we've been living together for a length of time which most married couples will never reach and we might as well face facts, we're lumbered with each other."

"Speak for yourself, Scotty."

"But I'm not really that interested in whether it could make things more straightforward financially — what I'm saying is, we could play a gig at our own wedding breakfast. We could tip off the papers and the TV, they'd love it. It's an 'angle' isn't? Two straight blokes getting married — and by the way, they're in a fucking great rock n roll band."

Scott could detect the changes in Will's facial expression. From horror to bemusement to deep consideration to a wide-eyed look of calculated interest.

"Yeah, but can two straight blokes form a civil partnership? Is it allowed?"

"I don't know for certain but think about it. If two gay blokes go to the registrar's office and say they want a civil partnership ceremony, the registrar is not going to ask them for proof that they're gay, is she?"

"I don't know. Maybe they inspect the house for copies of Attitude magazine or, I don't know, impeccable interior design."

"Seriously, though."

"I suppose not. But, but ..."

"But what?"

"Well, I certainly don't want people thinking we're a gay couple."

"Why would it matter? You always claim you're liberal."

"It's not that so much, I just wouldn't want people thinking I'd have bad enough taste to want to bum you."

"Don't flatter yourself in to thinking that you'd be the sort of gay I'd go for either."

"You would, you'd love a bit of me."

"The idea's got merit, though, admit it," said Scott.

"Yeah but if we're saying we're two gays having a civil partnership, that's not a story is it? That's not a publicity stunt. According to you, we're going to publicise the fact that we're two straight men getting hitched."

"But I don't see how they'd be able to stop us. We've lived together for 17 years, why shouldn't we have a civil partnership? There must be celibate gays who get married. You see old queens doing it, don't you? We probably wouldn't even have to kiss each other after we've exchanged rings."

"For fuck's sake, Scotty, you've been thinking about this too deeply."

"I've been thinking about how we're going to get a recording contract."

"You've been thinking about bumming me, I reckon."

"I'll get the Jack out," said Scott and poured them each a glass of JD and Coke.

There was silence in the flat. Scott downed his drink swiftly. Will started perusing the gatefold vinyl album cover of *Electric Ladyland* and lit up a Marlboro.

"I'd have this one who looks a bit like Carol Vorderman," said Will. "You'd have Hendrix himself, you little bum boy."

"You know it," said Scott. "You know this is the best idea either of us has had in years."

"True. It might just be your moment of genius. I've always suspected you'd be capable of one. Even though you've kept your ingenuity pretty well hidden all these years."

Scott smiled, he opened another can of Coke and added it to a further measure of whiskey. Then he ripped the ring-pull from the top of the Coke can.

Because they'd shared this bleak little space for half a lifetime, Will now knew exactly what his flatmate was thinking.

"Do it," said Will.

"You should do it, you reckon you'd be the dominant one. You'd wear the trousers."

"No, it was your idea, you do it."

"For fuck's sake," Scott laughed.

"On your knees, bitch."

Will stood and Scott, on one knee, took his flatmate's left hand in his own right.

"Will you marry me, Will?" he asked.

Will shook his head but said: "Yeah, go on then, you twat – but it's divorce if the band haven't been signed within six months."

Then Scott squeezed the Coke-can ring-pull over the knuckle of the ring finger on Will's left hand.

"This calls for a celebration," said will. "I haven't eaten any fresh fruit or veg for a fortnight. I'm going to catch scurvy. Let's go to the Wimpy and have a banana longboat."

14

FRESH WHITE LINEN

"What does heaven smell like?" Mabel asked her father.

"Well, how would I know? I've never been to heaven."

"Yet."

"Well, that's if you believe in heaven."

"Do you believe in heaven?"

"I'm not so sure."

These were not the kind of answers a seven-year-old girl wanted. Vague answers. Disinterested answers. Distracted answers. His damned Blackberry felt not so much a ball-and-chain connecting him to his office, rather an instrument of mental torture. Afternoons such as these ought to have been precious. Sacred. But there was never a day off, never a free moment to teach his daughter about life's little mysteries. As if he might know any more than she, anyway.

Even on an afternoon when the sun was injecting bodies with shots of pure vitamin, as it shimmered off the distant London skyline, the smartphone would not allow him to experience the simple pleasure of relaxing with his only child. And when you messaged people, it automatically boasted to the recipient on your behalf 'sent from my Blackberry mobile device'. Look at me, how impressive am I? I'm always on the go. Always working. No time here for discussing ethereal scents with schoolgirls. And daisy chains? Daisy chains are for drop-outs. Switchers-off. Part-timers.

"Well, imagine, Daddy, make-believe. What would heaven smell like?"

She sounded like an adult and he a child with attention-deficit issues. The thought of this jolted his brain back into daddy mode.

"Maybe heaven smells like different things to different people. I'm sure if there is a heaven, it's that sort of a magical place."

This was more like it. Mabel smiled.

"What would heaven smell like to you then, Daddy?"

"Well, in the morning it would smell like freshly ground coffee. In the daytime, hmmm, in the daytime, I think it would smell like tarmac, you know from the roadworks, fresh tarmac in the hot sun. And at night time it would definitely smell like fresh white linen bed sheets. Mummy's always changing the bed sheets – I love it when there's clean bed sheets."

"I think you like stronger smells than I do. Apart from the bed sheets. But those are good answers. Just because I don't agree with them all doesn't mean they're not good answers. You think heaven smells fresh but different fresh smells at different times of day. That's imaginatiative."

"Imaginative."

"Yes. Exactly."

"What would heaven smell like to you then, Mabs?"

"If I could choose. Well, it would taste like sticky toffee pudding ice-cream, you knew that, and it would probably smell like Mummy's perfume, I suppose. That or the doughnuts at the seaside. Possibly it would taste AND smell like the doughnuts at the seaside. But I'd like it to smell like Mummy's perfume, best of all."

"Actually, I probably should have said Mummy's perfume. If Mummy asks, say I said heaven would smell like her perfume."

"You want me to lie to Mummy?" said Mabel, smiling with genuine amusement but complete incredulity. This must have been her first introduction to the concept that one of her parents might be capable of lying to the other.

"Well, there are white lies, little fibs, to make people feel better. It's not a dirty, black lie to hurt people."

"Hmmm? That's not what they say at school. Miss just says all lying is wrong."

Teachers were so self-righteous, he decided. They were all on six weeks' holiday now and inflicting smart-arse comments like these on the rest of us, through our own children, while they were probably getting off their tits in Ibiza or supplementing their incomes by moonlighting as Burlesque dancers.

Mabel wore a summer dress, enthroned on the brow of the hill, surveying London from her suburban seat, like the child queen of the world. There was a haze, a smog, over the city, but fresh suburban air out here. It was very warm, a proper August day, like childhood Augusts, not the wet Augusts there'd been of late. They had fed deer, flung a frisbee, consumed ice-creams. He'd actually had a decent stab at this day-care caper, all in all. It hurt him that Mabel spent so much more time with her mother than with both of her parents together. And so very little time with he alone. She was Heather's daughter so much more than his – her speech, her mannerisms, her foibles, all her mother's. It almost made him resent his wife, resent women even. Mothers always spoke of 'juggling' careers and parenting. But what of fathers, who'd love the chance to juggle?

"Well, I guess you're right, I'm sure Mummy wouldn't want you to lie to me," he said, as he got back to work on the daisy chain. It wasn't until he undertook such an intricate task that he realised how much his hands shook, as if wired to the mains. A constant, perceptible motion, like the tiny vibrations of a humming fridge. He was wired with anxiety.

"She wouldn't ask me to fib to you," said Mabel. "I think she did once ask me not to tell you what happened but that's different to fibbing or lying. It's just not saying."

"Mummy asked you not to tell me something?"

"She TOLD me not to tell you."

"So I guess you wouldn't tell me what it was, then, if I asked."

"Well, not if Mummy told me not to. It was just something nice, a surprise for your birthday."

Mabel spoke breezily but noticed that her father was looking at her with intense seriousness.

"It's been my birthday now, though. My birthday was in April. And Mummy got me an iPad. It wasn't a surprise."

"Well, it must be for your next birthday because it wasn't as long ago as April."

Mabel counted on her fingers.

"April, May, June, July, August – yes it wasn't that long ago."

"It must be a wonderful surprise then if Mummy is planning something for my next birthday already, especially when there's Christmas to come before then."

There was a hint of crossness in his voice and Mabel sensed that she shouldn't have mentioned the surprise. Her bottom lip trembled and she began to sob. He pulled her close to him, dabbed at her tears with the fingers of one hand while tugging gently at her pigtails with the other.

"There's no need to cry, Mabs, I'm not angry. It's nice if Mummy has a birthday surprise for me. I certainly won't ask you what it is or else it would ruin the surprise."

Mabel fought back her tears and smiled.

"I'm sorry, baby."

He noticed the red light blinking on his Blackberry and felt it penetrating through his skull, squeezing the very matter of his brain. An email from Darren. A rare email these days.

Darren. The way he looked at Heather. The way that Darren and Heather barely spoke to each other when he was present any more. The way Darren kept avoiding his social calls. For the first 25 years of their friendship, Darren had always returned calls. And for the previous 15 years, Darren had always seemed capable of making perfectly natural small talk with Heather.

"And I won't ask Uncle Darren either, because if there's a secret, then I bet Uncle Darren will be involved somehow!"

He sounded cheerful to Mabel now. He sounded cheerful as he attempted to trick his seven-year-old daughter into divulging the secret which might lead to her own life being torn apart.

"That's all I actually know," Mabel smiled, reassured, "I don't even know what the surprise is. Just that Uncle Darren was on the phone talking about it to Mummy. But you'd already guessed Uncle Darren would be involved. He is your best friend."

"Well, yes. Anyway, we don't need to talk about this any more do we? We don't want Mummy to think that I know anything about what she is getting up to with Uncle Darren – we'd better head back to the car now, baby."

As they walked, hand in hand, down the hill, Mabel asked: "I wonder what heaven would smell like to Mummy? Shall we ask her?"

"Yes let's ask her. I often wonder what Mummy likes. We'll have to ask Mummy when we get home, won't we? We'll have to ask Mummy about her idea of heaven. And Uncle Darren when we next see him too."

15

SHEER WEIGHT OF TRAFFIC

'It's 7:17, we're a little late with the travel, but a big fanfare to welcome back Jack Bile from his holidays – how did the good folks get to work without you, this last fortnight Jackie baby? ...'

Just one patronising intro from Johnny Longson and the last fragment of clarity which had come from two weeks' leave had evaporated. The travel jingle lacerated Jack's brain. Then the apocalyptic comedy parping noises of the cartoon car horns. Then it was him. Him. Now. Talk, man.

And talk with a certain jauntiness combined with a sympathetic lightness of touch, appropriate to the bringing of bad news on a commercial radio station whose primary purpose is to massage minds into a soapy lather.

"Thanks, Johnny, just a few problems on the roads as rush hour begins to hot up and let's start with our dear old friend the M25. Anticlockwise, there's a broken-down vehicle in the roadworks just past Junction 21 for the M1, that's already causing some serious tailbacks. We can expect that to get worse over the next hour or so. And on the clockwise carriageway between junctions 11 and 12, leading up to the M3 intersection, there's a vehicle on fire, which has been moved to the hard shoulder. Not too much else to report on the motorways yet, but on the A1 northbound by the Angel of the North there's a lorry overturned and it's shed its load ... so delays of up to half an hour there ... JackBileLiveFMtravel!"

"A lorry's spilt its load, Jack?" asked Longson, with faux excitement, "What's the load then? Come on, sunshine, have you forgotten that this is your one opportunity to bring us a little joy, rather than just misery – a chance to get the texters texting in about a spilt load?"

A comedy spillage, Jack's greatest dread. He knew the load which was causing mayhem in the North East was several thousand tins of sweetcorn. But after seven years of this, he couldn't bear to read out the detail. He couldn't face the texters texting him puns about sweetcorn. He couldn't bear the false mirth it would evoke in Johnny Longson. Jack Bile only wanted death and destruction on the roads now. Multi-vehicle accidents. Air ambulances. Emergency services having to cut victims out of wreckages. Carnage. Only carnage would give him any sense of job satisfaction.

He only felt any hint of meaning in his work on those mornings when the M25 resembled the seventh circle of hell. Yet even then, true contentment was elusive. The genuine news could merely be hinted at. He could only commiserate with the minor inconveniences of the Audi filth, the White Van trash and the articulated psychopaths stuck in their tailbacks, rather than sympathise with the parents whose two daughters had been crushed to death on a dual carriageway. Tomorrow those sisters might make the actual news bulletins, once relatives had been informed, long after all lanes had been opened and barriers repaired. Then the story would have moved above his pay grade.

And if there was true carnage in the long hot summer, with delays of countless miles and several hours, it would often be reported that holidaymakers had erected deckchairs in the fast lane, tossed beachballs over stationary bonnets and played soft-tennis on the hard shoulder until the air ambulance arrived. Making a day of it, as their forefathers may have done, while spectating at public executions.

"Jack?"

It was him. Now. Talk, man.

Dead air on the airwaves. Dead air in his windpipe. Panic in his mind. Hatred in his soul.

And then, and then ...

"Well, you'd know all about spilt loads, Johnny."

What with you being the world's biggest wanker. He instantly assumed he would be getting a second written warning for this but why hadn't he simply had the guts to go the whole hog and call Johnny Longson 'the world's biggest wanker', live on national radio? Several hundred thousand years ago he had actually trained to be a journalist and he'd been told that 'fair comment' was an admissible defence in a libel case.

Jack hated to admit it but while Longson was smug and glib he was also a consummate pro at the tabloid end of the radio market. He effortlessly moved on to a sensitive phone interview about severe premen-strual tension, while simultaneously performing knife-across-the-throat gestures at his 'travel boy'. Burning with three-quarters-part rage and a quarter-part shame, Jack tried to out-eyeball the talk-show host. His resistance was short lived and the show's pro-ducer, a severe, institutionalised company man called Martyn with a Y, emailed him from the newsroom, de-manding that they speak immediately after his shift had finished.

Longson may have been the chief stimulus for Jack's hatred and rage but it was Martyn with a Y who had an even more corrosive effect on his soul. Martyn was Longson's apologist, the man who imposed LiveFM's status quo with a Stalinist zeal and a remarkable absence of humour. A man who, to the outsider, could not have appeared more ill-suited to a career at a light-entertainment commercial radio station. A man whose patronage kept Longson in position, their futures intertwined, their phony mutual fawning bordering on the obscene. The man who, more than anybody, had kept Jack Bile in his place – a thirty-second, twice-hourly slot chronicling the traffic jams of an overpopulated island with an insufficient road network.

* * * * *

When he'd arrived as LiveFM's new travel boy seven years earlier, the move had been regarded as a 'foot in the door' by Jack, by his girlfriend (now his fiancee) Lucinda (Cinda or Cinders, never Lucy), and by all of their family and friends. It was just the opening he needed to become a successful radio presenter, before moving into television. Jack had a good idea of when this career path had been cordoned-off, it was around the time Jonny Longson had ceased to see him as an ally and begun to regard him as a major irritant as well as some sort of threat. This almost certainly occurred on the night when Jack won a minor radio-industry award for being 'travel presenter of the year', whilst Longson had finished as runner-up in the far more prestigious 'best breakfast host' category – an award he'd won for the previous two years. The man who had dished out Jack's prize plaque had referred glowingly to the quality of Jack's 'banter' and referred to he and Longson as a 'double act'. Longson had reacted with open fury. And after that, all talk of Jack progressing up the slippery pole had ceased, as had plans for his wedding to Cinders.

It wasn't that Jack wanted to BE Johnny Longson; rather that he'd wanted to be a better, more decent version of the man. After seven years as travel boy, though, he had finally realised that he was never likely to be any sort of Johnny Longson, any sort of anchorman, chat-show presenter, phone-in host, minor TV celeb. Never destined to be what the industry referred to as the 'Talent'. Most people reach their glass ceilings in life, experience ultimate disappointments, accept limitations. In his more reflective moments, Jack Bile realised this. It was just that he was forced to spend every working day being taunted by his nemesis; witnessing Johnny Longson being feted and pampered, excused and indulged, as the 'Talent' always was.

Longson would even taunt Jack about Cinda; ever since the pair of them had met, and flirted, at a Christmas do. Occasionally even on air, disguised as friendly, laddish 'banter' – "You're looking tired this morning, Jackie, has the lovely Cinders been keeping you up?" "When are you going to make an honest woman of your Cinderella, eh Prince Charming?" Cinda always seemed to hear about these instances, feigned bemusement but clearly felt a deep sense of flattery. How Jack Bile now loathed the concept of 'banter', even the mere mention of the word. And how he despised Johnny Longson.

The LiveFM studio was a dark, windowless place, in literal terms. For Jack Bile, it had long since become a dark, windowless place in any term imaginable.

Sometimes, when the traffic news was quiet, when the information from the police and the AA was scant, he would find himself not just wishing for death crashes but imagining specific scenes of destruction, in his daydreams, then later in his fretful dreams at night. At first occasionally, but increasingly often, remarkably similarly pictures began to appear before his eyes on the Highways Agency cameras.

He had kept quiet about this phenomenon, if indeed it wasn't just a series of coincidences, for some months. He couldn't tell Cinda for fear that she might genuinely believe he was cracking up, especially as his increasingly short temper and lengthening periods of quiet rage had already been troubling her.

Yet when Jack awoke in the middle of the night with a chilling premonition of a family of five being wiped out in a multi-vehicle pile-up – and heard of the same thing having happened within an hour of arriving at work the next morning – Jack knew he would have to tell somebody and that somebody would probably have to be his only friend at Live FM, the weatherman Ben Dooley.

This had been about 18 months earlier, not long before Ben had found his escape route. A qualified meteorologist, he decided to set himself up, effectively, as a rogue weather forecaster, who'd sell invented weather-related scare stories to the tabloids. By now, the newspapers were lapping up his fictitious tales, in particular one middle-market newspaper which often used to ring Ben and demand something for a front-page splash – snow at Christmas, snow in summer, global warming was causing Armageddon, global warming was a myth, a freak heatwave which would kill dogs – anything which might frighten their elderly readership. Jack wondered whether he could set up a similar freelance operation for traffic news but unlike the weather, there was no real science to the traffic, the margin for bullshit was far too limited.

Ben had also established a sideline in starting and spreading urban myths. This was less profitable than rogue weather forecasting, indeed there seemed no way of truly making it pay, but it was far more rewarding. The most successful take-up for one of Ben's myths was the 'fact' that US federal agents used the song *System Addict* by the 1980s pop group Five Star to torture detainees at Guantanamo. This rumour had become so widely accepted as fact that Ben had heard TV defence experts referring to it on news bulletins. Somewhere along the line, somebody had added the detail that agents used to play the whole of Five Star's *Silk and Steel* album before realising that playing System Addict on a continuous loop was far more effective for the crushing of Islamic spirit.

And this fantasy was a product of the mind of Ben Dooley, the only person Jack felt able to confide in. Not perhaps the sort of mind he'd ideally have chosen for reassurance of his own sanity but such was the media world – a place of ego and eccentricity masking rampant insecurity, both personal and professional. Ben, Jack believed, was perhaps the only man who might be capable of understanding him. So they had ensconced themselves in the snug bar of The Rampant Horse after the end of their shifts, as they had done approximately once a week for the previous four years. Yet Jack never previously had anything significant to say to Ben; nor Ben to Jack. Their drinking sessions had consisted largely of bitching, piss-taking and backbiting; about Johnny Longson, any of Live FM's other 'talent', Martyn with a Y, the other producers or the station controller.

So it wasn't until halfway through their second pint, that Jack had even dared to voice his obsession.

"Ben, you know those daft films and mini-series where spooky kids keep saying 'I see dead people' and all that?"

"Yeah, I hate that sort of shit."

"Yeah, me too, it's just that, well, I, I do. I do see dead people, mate. I do actually see dead people."

"Yeah, on the traffic cameras?"

"No, mate, I see the dead people in my head – then the same dead people on the traffic cameras."

Ben laughed: "You silly twat."

"It's not a wind-up."

"Okay, the rule – the unwritten but incontrovertible rule – is that if you deny it's a wind-up twice and then it turns out to actually be a wind-up, then there's no disgrace on me and you just end up looking like a twat."

"Okay right. It's not a wind-up. I have premonitions about people dying in traffic accidents and then I see them on the screen."

"And you know the rule?"

"I know the rule and I'm serious."

"Fuck. You're not about to tell me you've seen me in a car wreck are you?"

"No I'm not. This isn't about YOU. I really needed to tell somebody. It's becoming a bit, like I say, spooky. Terrifying, really."

"Have you seen anyone you actually know yet?"

"No."

"Well, look on the bright side, pal, you might see Longson mangled to death before long."

Jack smiled, without conviction.

"I'm serious, though, mate. I can't tell Cinda, she already thinks I'm losing the plot."

"How many times has this happened?"

"Five or six."

"Jesus, I thought you were the only sane one working in that place, mate. Sounds like you're as mad as the rest of them.

"Yeah, thanks mate. I do feel kind of sane in every other respect."

"Which is like the Yorkshire Ripper saying 'yeah, but there are lots of prostitutes I DIDN'T kill.'"

"You think I should see a shrink or something?"

"I don't know mate, they might section you."

"You're not being a great help."

"Well, I don't know, I dream of weather maps. Maybe it just goes with the job. You're bound to dream about work. And your work features a lot of dead people in cars. I tell you what, though, I was going to ask for some pork scratchings with the next round but I've lost my appetite now."

And that was, effectively, that. Ben began to refer to Jack as 'Psycho'. Jack continued to experience accurate premonitions. Ben left the station. And Jack's life moved on at the pace of the M25 in the Friday night rush-hour when a lorry had shed its load and a comedy spillage had closed two lanes.

* * * * *

It didn't help that Jack slept so little, that he feared sleep, dreaded the images it would bring, and so never quite drifted off. His body would simply shut down whenever he reached the point of total exhaustion, then abruptly jolt itself awake after not nearly enough sleep. An insomniac can never imagine a harsher curse than insomnia. No peace for the wicked, no sleep for the damned.

Cinda, unlike most women, always slept like a baby. She was rarely aware that her fiancé had been pacing the house or sitting on the sofa watching cable with the volume turned down. Soft porn or American sports. He had never had much interest in sports and did not even possess a vague understanding of the American ones. Yet the choreographed movements of the brick-shithouse shoulder-padded rugby types; the pinstriped rounders players; the black netball giants in their technicolor vests; those psychotic stick-wielding ice skaters – these all seemed strangely therapeutic. By contrast, the fucking of the porn stars merely seemed ridiculous, a source of minor amusement. His libido had long since faded, if indeed he could ever have been aroused by such unrealistic people having such unrealistic sex.

If he still hadn't fallen asleep by 2.30am, Jack chain-smoked and drank coffee until just before 5am when his alarm would have sounded. He'd slip into bed at 4.55am and convinced Cinda he'd been sleeping for hours.

He wasn't sure what his motive was for this pretense. He didn't know why he couldn't admit his anxieties and tensions to the woman he loved. Except that he was undoubtedly in awe of her. He knew Cinda outranked him on every imaginable category of the relationship *Top Trumps* card. Looks, salary, breeding, health, sociability, sense of humour. So he supposed he feared that any sign of weakness might make her reconsider. Not that Cinda wasn't already doubting the significance of the diamond ring on her finger, the one he really couldn't afford, as his moods became ever bleaker, the longer he read the traffic news on LiveFM.

Jack had never enjoyed driving. He held no interest in cars, to a quite remarkable degree, given his career.

He knew nothing of their workings, of their makes or models. He saw no beauty in even the most expensive varieties. They held no more aesthetic value to him than a fridge or a washing-machine. He hadn't taken driving lessons at seventeen like most of his contemporaries. He had waited until his early twenties when, employed by a local newspaper, a driving licence had become a necessity. And since being a 'travel boy' he had gradually developed something approaching a full-blown phobia of driving, of roads, of traffic. It appeared to him a tortuous experience. He was not surprised that those who drove trucks or minicabs for a living were the most likely to become serial killers. He felt certain such a life would make him homicidal too.

'DON'T DRIVE TIRED' ordered the motorway matrix signs, then 'DON'T PHONE WHILE DRIVING'. You'd surely have to do one or the other, at least, unless those totalitarians in control of the matrix signs wished to insert more hours into the day.

Jack often imagined himself falling asleep as he drove to the Tube station. Or of being sent spinning across the oncoming carriageway by a fellow driver, who had passed out at the wheel, himself shattered by overwork. Or hurtling inexorably into a pile-up after the woman three cars in front had taken her eyes off the road while sending an SMS apologising to her husband for being late out of the office, because her colleague had needed to stay at home to mind a sick daughter and had been unable to pay a child-minder. A car crashing into a car, crashing into another car. A life hurtling into a life, hurtling into another life.

Yet we trusted them all, as they piloted their 80mph steel sculptures beside us, behind us, ahead of us. The car in front is a Toyota. The driver in front has an overloaded mind which is failing to compute the sight of brake lights. A wonder it did not happen more often. A wonder anybody ever got anywhere safely any more.

These feelings, these fears, were not premonitions, not in the same vein as the car-crash images. This was not the way Jack felt he was destined to die. The manner of his own death remained a mystery. These were merely the rational fears of a man who was physically and mentally spent. An air ambulance circling his mind. Sheer weight of traffic grinding him to a halt.

* * * * *

There had been two weeks of peace and complacency on holiday. At times he had even felt like himself – his distant self – the one Cinda had presumably fallen for many years before. They had shared bottles of rosé and meals for two, played cards and even made love once or twice.

But that previous night, not long after he had fallen asleep, Jack had been jump-started back into consciousness. An image of a woman's face. Pale except for a scarlet stream seeping from a head wound. Peaceful then shrouded by a member of the emergency services. Grainy images, as if on a CCTV camera. Had it been Cinda? He couldn't be sure.

Even after Martyn had dispatched his doom-laden email, demanding to speak to him about his on-air barb at Longson, Jack fretted about Cinda. He fought the urge to send her a text, asking whether she had arrived at work safely, something he had not done since the earliest days of their relationship. Then he recalled another image, of a suited man with grey skin,

231

disfigured horribly, his body moulded by glass and metal. These later recollections of a previous night's dream were somehow more troubling than those which revealed themselves instantly. Especially as he would be due back on air again shortly, with Longson smiling cruelly at him. Jack could only avert his gaze. Downtrodden, humiliated, vanquished.

"And now it's over to Jack Bile, the National Radio Industry Awards travel presenter of the year 2008 ..."

It had been five years since the fleeting triumph of that awards night. Jack couldn't even have told you in which year he'd won his little plaque. But the date was firmly etched on the mind of Longson. The year in which he had finished as runner-up in the 'best breakfast host' category after two previous victories. Of course Longson would have remembered the date.

"Thanks Johnny, thanks for that reminder of former glories," Jack focused on his computer screen and microphone, adopting his Live FM on-air persona, like a familiar musty old overcoat in need of a dry-clean. "Well, first some better news on the A1 northbound – the shed load has been cleared away now and all lanes are open. As you were asking earlier, Johnny, it was a load of sweetcorn. So a chance for you texters to text in there. But don't make those puns too corny, geddit?"

As Jack continued with worsening news about the M25 anticlockwise in Hertfordshire, the self-loathing welled up inside him. He was playing the management's game again now. Interactivity. Dreadful puns. Light entertainment for the braindead masses. Realising this, Longson was curling up a nostril and shaking his head, slowly and deliberately. Utter contempt in his eyes, then the slightest hint of a victorious smirk. He'd be on the telly later that evening, co-presenting a lowbrow prime-time consumer show. Jack knew that Cinda would make a point of watching it, Provided that she had not been killed on her journey to work. He suspected that Cinda's insistence on tuning in to watch Longson was malicious. She had never been overly sympathetic when her fiance had spoken of his loathing for the breakfast show host. She did not challenge Jack about his lack of career progression nor his overwhelming bitterness. He often wished that she would. Her silent disappointment was more crushing than a debate on those issues could ever have been.

"Thanks Jack, another potential award-winner there. One for the nominations medley, I'm sure. And as Jack said there, you can text in your puns about the sweetcorn spillage in the North East to the usual number. I know Jack looks forward to a little levity in proceedings ..."

Jack looked into Longson's eyes, ruefully, inviting pity. He had lost the will to fight with the minor multi-media celeb, he wished only for some sort of mercy, some let-up. From across the desk and between the monitors, Longson bit his bottom lip and narrowed his eyes. 'I've got you, you little bastard, I've done you like a kipper,' his expression said.

There was an almost imperceptible lifting of the gloom once Longson finished his show at 10am. Travel boys, though, had to keep proper working hours, so Jack's shift consisted of both the breakfast show and the mid-morning phone-in programme which followed it. Jack was barely aware of the nature of this following show, as he robotically scanned for updates on the AA feed and the police information services. From the seeping discharges of noise which had permeated his consciousness, among those cacophonous upbeat advert jingles usually based on football chants, it seemed that the topic for the phone-in debate was the concept that political correctness had indeed gone mad. In fact, whatever the original topic for debate had been, all conversational roads on the mid-morning phone-in show invariably led to this subject and never deviated thereafter.

And you couldn't simply broadcast to people any more. Jack even had to accept information from eye-witnesses and rubber-neckers on the roads. Interactivity was the curse of the age. Phone-ins, social media, message boards. Everybody needed to have a voice. Even though the vast majority of them didn't possess the basic intelligence required to deserve one.

Jack Bile's only opportunity for revenge on LiveFM's pond-life listenership was a brief half-hourly window in which to sentence them to the soul-destroying desperation of a lengthy tailback or circuitous detour. He finally clocked off at 1pm, with not so much a sense of relief as a cocktail of cravings. Cravings for alcohol, for nicotine, for daylight, for relaxation. Most of all, for the elusive destination of peaceful sleep.

Yet before the chance for any of that, there would be Martyn. An appointment with the undead. An invitation had been issued to join Martyn in his office. Which was more of a cubicle really. Had Martyn been prone to cat-swinging – a pastime for which he possessed the necessary cruelty but insufficient flamboyance – then this would have been no place to indulge in it.

Martyn fidgeted in his seat, manoeuvring a pencil around his middle finger. First against his index finger, then against his ring finger, then back again. This twirling was the nearest thing to a display of animation he ever really mustered within the working environment these days. There had been karaoke once, many years before, but it had ended in humiliation. Martyn tumbling backwards from the stage at the climax to 'Sweet Caroline'. Roars of amusement from subordinates; significant head -shaking from a member of the company board. Martyn had been virtually teetotal ever since, attempting and failing to seek different pleasures elsewhere. His skin had grown greyer, its worry lines more pronounced. Besides a computer monitor and keyboard, there was only a disfigured rubber stress ball and a long-neglected Newton's cradle on the desk. No click-clacking of metal upon metal to ease the passage of time. No opportunity for mirth here, Jack realised, little leeway for forgiveness. He was not even afforded the courtesy of eye contact.

"You wanted to see me, Martyn?"

"Yes, yes, I did, Jack. About the spilt load – and before you interject, I am not as immune to irony or sarcasm or puerile attempts at humour as you imagine I am, so please don't try to persuade me that there was no double meaning in your little put-down."

And Jack had to concede that he had been outflanked. His only gameplan had been to insist that his comment had been entirely innocent.

"I didn't think it would be obvious to the listeners, Martyn. I honestly don't believe it was too blatant."

"If a dry old stick like me understood exactly what you meant then I'm sure many of our listeners would have detected it too. Indeed, we've had several emails on the subject. You think Johnny Longson is a wanker, that much is clear. It is clear to Johnny, who was absolutely livid with you when he saw me after coming off air today and I can't say I blame him. Your job, as you know, is to inform the listeners and to support the host, not to undermine him, whatever your opinion of him."

"I do apologise, Martyn."

"I'd move you if I could, Jack. If there were any feasible job swaps, I'd move you to an afternoon or evening slot. Even the graveyard. Because your antipathy for Johnny has become a huge problem."

"I appreciate your words, Martyn, and I can assure you that I'll learn from this. There's really no need to underline the point with disciplinary action, I assure you."

And Jack Bile listened to himself pleading for clemency from a boss he held in such low esteem, so that he could continue to hold down a job which he detested. He listened to himself as if there had been an echo on a phone line. He listened to his own pathetic predicament. Had he possessed more energy, he may have lashed out in anger at Martyn, at Longson, at Live FM, at the world at large. Instead, his anger would only turn inwardly.

"I could hand you a written warning, Jack, which would be your second – and, of course, your final warning. That's the very least I could do."

Jack had not perceived his on-air comment as a sackable offence until now but as Martyn's lips grew thinner and his skin turned greyer still, he began to realise that the old zombie was considering his dismissal.

"Well, I'd accept that warning, Martyn, I understand that my actions merit it."

Martyn clenched the stress ball inside the fist of his right hand.

"Yes I am sure you would, Jack. But I fear that your

working relationship with Johnny is no longer tenable ..."

Oh. Here we go, then. The P45. The plastic crate for his possessions and dear old Joe, the harmless security guy, frog-marching him out of the building. This is how it would end, after all this time. This realisation, though, seemed to shine a light deep inside his mind.

Martyn was pausing, perhaps unnerved by the realisation that Jack was now staring at him intently. A wry smile appeared on the travel boy's lips. A distant sense of relief in his eyes. At least that is what Martyn read in Jack's expression. But then Martyn was indeed a dry old stick. He could not read Jack Bile's mind. He wasn't even close to computing the thoughts behind that expression, from the opposite side of his cubicle's desk. How could he even begin to comprehend that his subordinate was slowly piecing together the fragments of a dreadful nightmare and assembling them into a very real vision of the future?

"I'm sorry, Martyn, but you're going to die."

"What? Jack, are you issuing me with some sort of death threat?"

"No, Martyn, it's not a threat. I'm not going to kill you. It will have nothing to do with me. I'm just warning you that you are going to die in a road traffic accident, and it's going to happen some time very soon, so if you need to tie up any loose ends – wills, life insurance policies, funeral arrangements – you had better act quickly. I'm sorry to be the bearer of bad news but I guess that's been my purpose around here these last seven years. JackBileLiveFMtravel!"

Martyn's fist relinquished the stress ball, which bounced unevenly out of the cubicle. He began to sweat heavily and his eyes narrowed.

"Jack, you are clearly in need of some sort of professional help ..."

"As are you, Martyn, as I said; a lawyer, a life-insurance salesman, an undertaker ..."

"I can only regard your words to be some sort of death threat and I must ask security to escort you from the building. You will hear from the HR department soon. I will also have to consider whether I call the police about this. I regret that your time with LiveFM has had to end this way."

"There will always be other jobs for me, Martyn. It's your family I feel for. It is possible that your wife will also be killed. I certainly envisage a woman in the car with you and she will sustain serious head injuries, at the very least. I understand that this is not your average travel bulletin. You normally prefer us to be a little more reactive and less proactive in these matters."

Martyn rose to his feet and leant forward as if he were about to grab Jack by the throat but the younger man remained seated and smiled benignly at his elder.

"Security!" yelled Martyn.

"It's ok, Martyn, I'll arrange for old Joe to escort me out, I know the basic procedure. There's very little in my desk to clear, one of the smaller plastic crates should suffice. You have far more important matters to deal with. I refer, of course, to your imminent death. I apologise again for having to inform you but I'm sure if you take heed, then you will appreciate the heads-up."

* * * * *

As he left the office, Jack bade farewell and offered his best wishes to old Joe, who had barely frog-marched him at all, merely guided him to the exit door with a gentle hand in the small of his back. Jack deposited the small crate and its meagre contents into an industrial bin as he blinked in the sunlight of a cloudless English summer's afternoon. Just a five-minute stroll towards the south bank of the Thames and he would even benefit from a cooling breeze off the river. There, small children cavorted in the fountains, others rode a carousel, tourists browsed through shoddy souvenirs and teenagers frottaged in the heat. These fleeting sights of freedom pleased him. There really would be much to enjoy. Less money, yes, but so much more time. This would turn out to be, Jack believed, the best thing which could ever have happened to him.

He would have to tell Cinda soon enough, he supposed, but not today and not that evening either. Instead, he switched off his phone and enjoyed the loosening of every sinew in his back and neck. The cessation of the throbbing in his temples. The relief of the soreness in his eyes. He bought an over-priced juice and felt the goodness infuse him, from the fruit, from the sun, from the fresh air.

He strolled north across the river and west towards the great parks. Bare flesh sprawled there, offered up in worship, reddening in the glow. Deckchairs dotted throughout the hectares. Handstands around the bandstand. The scent of melting vanilla and *Ambre Solaire* on the breeze. As he lay, the storm-clouds in Jack's mind were scattered. In their place, a soothing haze.

During the two hours in which Jack sunbathed, Martyn would be killed on the southern section of the M25.

Likewise his passenger, Janine the secretary, with

whom he had been having a miserable, oppressive extramarital affair. Martyn would only just have begun to tell Janine about the rantings of Jack Bile, when he would fail to spot the indicator lights of the haulage truck, moving out into the middle lane in frustration at a meandering caravan. The truck driver would never forget the sight of the debris. A symbolic image of a shredded, blown-out tyre would always haunt him. But the truck driver would be absolved of all blame. Witnesses would suggest that he had given Martyn plenty of time to react. Martyn's fury at Jack Bile's unhinged behaviour would cause his fateful lapse in concentration. Janine would not even get to hear of Jack's premonition about the death or serious injury of a female passenger before she would receive massive, fatal head injuries of her own. Martyn would only realise the truth in Jack's words for a split-second before his own death.

Crash-scene investigators were baffled as to why his airbag did not activate. It was as if some terrible preordained fate had been at play. Martyn's company car was top of the range, not a year old and with only ten thousand miles on the clock.

News of the lengthy tailbacks on the M25, due to the temporary closure of the motorway shortly before rush hour, would be broadcast by LiveFM's afternoon travel girl, hours before employees of the radio station would receive any indication that the senior producer of their flagship breakfast show had caused the accident and perished along with another company employee.

Martyn had made no phone calls, no adjustments to his will, no checks on the details of his life insurance policy. The funeral would have to be guesswork. He had never expressed any opinions on religion, except for a vague agnosticism. In the past, he'd enjoyed both Church of England burials and lighter humanist affairs in crematoria. And Martyn truly had enjoyed funerals; at least more so than most other social occasions. Wakes brought out the best in him; polite platitudes, vol-au-vents eaten over napkins, the dispensation of meaningless sympathy.

Martyn's wife would be too devastated by the presence of Janine in the passenger seat to put any great thought into the funeral arrangements. Her tears would flow from a sense of bitterness and betrayal, rather than grief or loss. Martyn's name would be misspelt 'Martin' on the printed notices directing mourners to the correct crematorium chapel. His wife would even consider having it deliberately misspelt on his headstone, such had been her irritation at the phrase 'Martyn with a Y' over the previous 25 years.

Johnny Longson would read a eulogy so dreadfully insincere that members of the LiveFM hierarchy would begin to wonder whether the breakfast show's steadily decreasing audience figures could only be reversed by a change of host. This notion would be whispered to Martyn's successor at the wake, prompting a genuine, thoughtful nodding of the head. He would leave a memo to himself on his mobile phone. Longson would now be on borrowed time.

Jack Bile wouldn't attend the funeral. It would be another warm, pleasant day and so he would return to the park, roll out a thin blanket, rub in some lotion and doze peacefully in the heat. As they closed the curtains around Martyn's coffin, Jack would be slipping slowly into a now-familiar, welcome sleep, lulled by the tunes of children's laughter and birdsong.

The sounds of the traffic around Hyde Park Corner, even the occasional blaring of an angry horn, would remain faintly audible to him. But it would be distant now; nothing but meaningless, harmless background noise.

ACKNOWLEDGMENTS

Many thanks to Matt Trollope, without whom these stories would have been sitting on my laptop for eternity. His hard work and devotion in editing the book has gone far beyond the call of duty. Likewise thanks to Mick Walsh, whose expert eye in proof-reading was a godsend. They have both been far too generous with their time.

Thanks to those in newspapers who gave me belief that I was worth reading: Paul Ridley, Ted Chadwick, Pete Butcher, Sheelagh Bree and James Brown among them.

To Dave Spring, whose spirit must feature somewhere in *All Our Bonfires*. A kind friend who is greatly missed.

Love and thanks to Kat, Emily and Bethany. To Dad for persuading me to love books in the first place. To Mum for the squirrels and to James for the washing machines.

Dave Kidd
Essex, July 2014

ABOUT THE AUTHOR

Dave Kidd was born in Essex in 1974. He has been a national newspaper sports writer since 1996 and is currently Chief Sports Writer at the *Sunday Mirror* and a columnist for the *Daily Mirror*. He is married with one daughter, one son and one stepdaughter. *Half Man Half Misfit* is his first published work of fiction.

www.ingramcontent.com/pod-product-compliance
Lightning Source LLC
Chambersburg PA
CBHW060548260626
47161CB00003B/1109